Barrettsport Mysteries

I0683287

A
BODY
in the
SACRISTY

Alan Kemister

Acknowledgements:

I posted the first draft on theNextBigWriter, an online writing community and workshop in 2013. JP Lundstrum, Judy Suchan, Don Chambers, Nathan B Childs and FlowingPencil persevered, offering comments on chapters from the first to the last. Their help, and that of many others who read one or many chapters, was invaluable. Four years and many revisions later, I have a much-improved manuscript those early reviewers might hardly recognize.

I have also benefitted from the friendship and encouragement I received from the members of two Halifax area writing communities, the Evergreen Writers Group and the Bedford Writers Circle. The Evergreen group encouraged my initial efforts to publish short stories. I now have fourteen published stories, including ones in two anthologies produced by the Evergreen Writers Group—*Out of the Mist: 22 Atlantic Canadian Ghost Stories*, and *Off Highway: Journeys of Nova Scotia Writers*. Without this grounding, I would never have completed a novel. Cathy MacKenzie, Janet McGinity and Tom Robson read and commented on a nearly final draft of *A Body in the Sacristy*, and others in both groups have commented on one or more chapters.

I could not have finished this project without the freely offered help of all these people.

Finally, I thank my loving wife of forty-five years for ignoring the hours I spent slouching in front of my computer when I should have been doing something useful, for putting up with the piles of research material I left strewn about the house, and for providing a final pass through the manuscript looking for those niggling mistakes authors always miss.

Map of Barrettsport and Environs

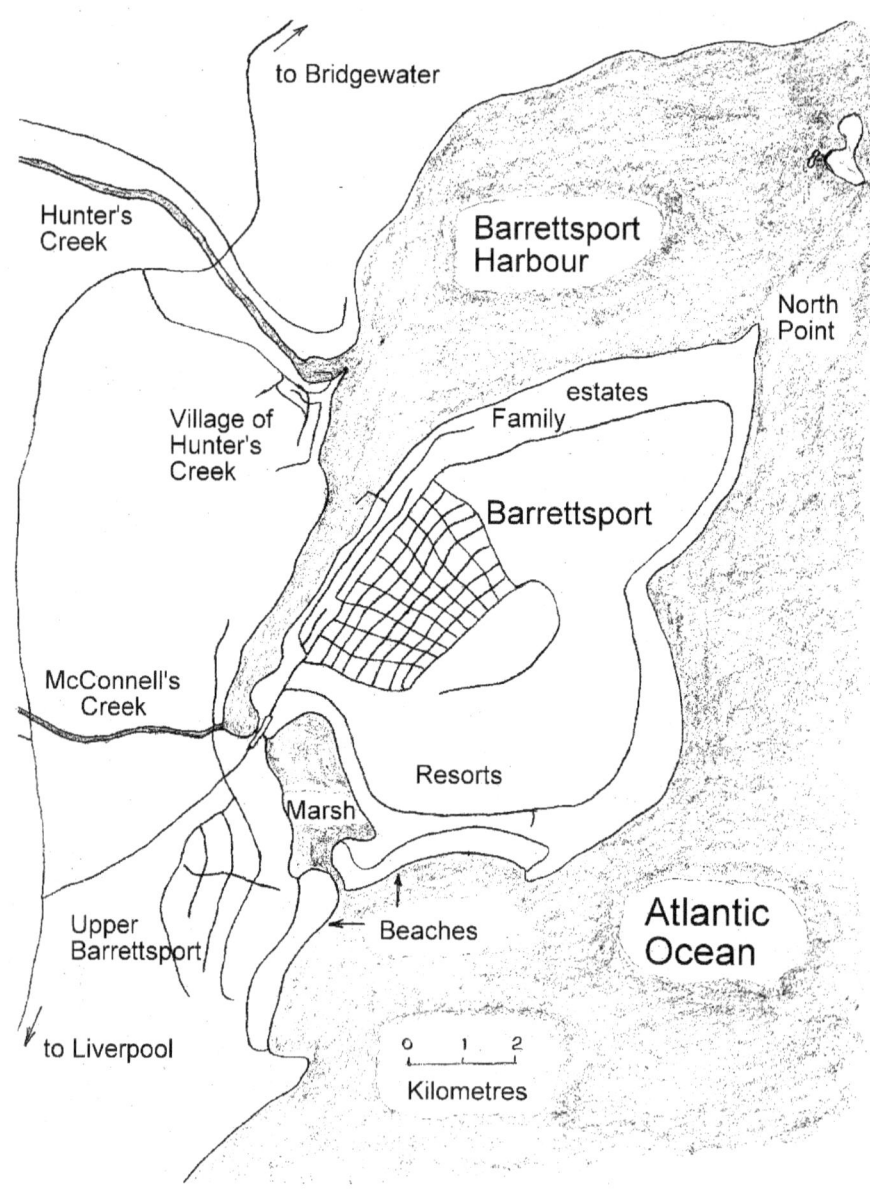

to Bridgewater

Hunter's Creek

Barrettsport Harbour

North Point

Village of Hunter's Creek

estates

Family

Barrettsport

McConnell's Creek

Resorts

Marsh

Atlantic Ocean

Upper Barrettsport

Beaches

to Liverpool

0   1   2
Kilometres

4

Barrettsport street map with locations of places featured in the text

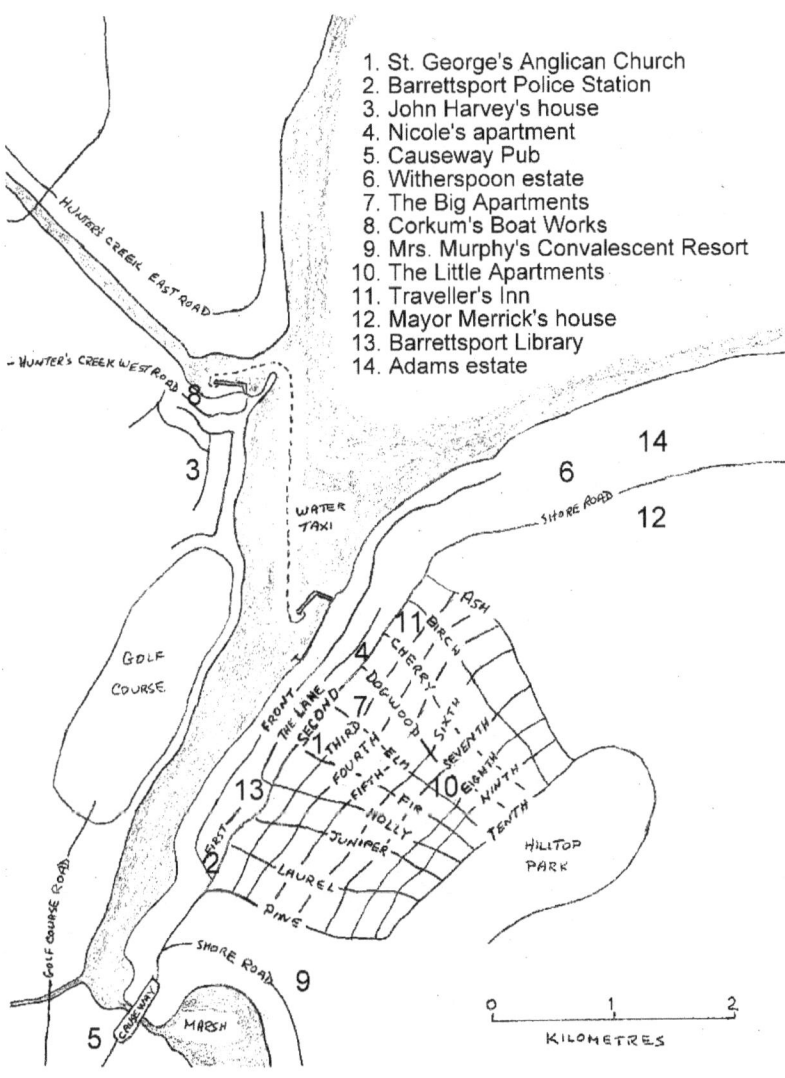

1. St. George's Anglican Church
2. Barrettsport Police Station
3. John Harvey's house
4. Nicole's apartment
5. Causeway Pub
6. Witherspoon estate
7. The Big Apartments
8. Corkum's Boat Works
9. Mrs. Murphy's Convalescent Resort
10. The Little Apartments
11. Traveller's Inn
12. Mayor Merrick's house
13. Barrettsport Library
14. Adams estate

5

Chapter One

Newly recruited Detective Simon Goodyear refused to let the cold, dreary springtime weather on Canada's Atlantic coast deter him from his early morning run. He ran from his Third Street apartment to the waterfront and along Front Street to a rocky beach at the edge of town. From the beach, he followed a path to Shore Road and on to the North Point Lighthouse. As he pounded through the omnipresent fog, Simon wondered if moving east had been such a bright idea. It was the age-old question people asked themselves after committing to major changes in their lives. Had his relocation to Barrettsport, Nova Scotia been a smart move?

After a decade on a large police force in a dynamic Canadian city, he'd relished the opportunity for a fresh start in a smaller community. Simon hadn't left his old job in disgrace, but five years on the drug squad working the unfriendly streets of Vancouver's Downtown Eastside had sapped his enthusiasm. He'd become a cog in a machine, unable to provide citizens with the personalized help that attracted him to police work.

A raid that resulted in serious injury to a colleague and the pointless deaths of two young women galvanized his resolve. He began searching in earnest for a position on a smaller force where he could help his friends and neighbours. The Barrettsport job seemed like the ideal solution.

Barrettsport was Nova Scotia's tenth largest town, and one of the few with its own police force. It was an unusual place with an independent-minded population that didn't rely on fishing or boat building to stoke its economic engines. The economy depended on upscale tourists at

7

exclusive resort hotels and five wealthy families who treated the town as their private fiefdom. Their sense of grandeur produced a community reminiscent of a New England resort from the roaring twenties.

After Chief of Police Reginald DeWolfe convinced the town fathers he could no longer combine the duties of chief and detective, Simon became Barrettsport's only detective. During his first month on his new job, Simon completed several minor investigations the chief passed on to him and spent many hours becoming familiar with the town. To date, he'd not had a case he could call his own.

*****

Later that morning, Jim Ellis strode to the Great West Doors of St. George's Anglican Church. The edifice was too pretentious for a town with fewer than four thousand residents, but a magnificent building reflecting Barrettsport's distinctive character.

Inside the church, Jim shook the fog from his Tilley hat and stripped off his oilskin jacket, revealing a small man in his mid-sixties. The clean-shaven volunteer neatly dressed in blue jeans and tartan work shirt was eager to attack an intriguing carpentry problem. A counter in the sacristy—the church's repository for wine, vestments, and vessels used in services—rested on a sealed cabinet. Deciding how to gain access to the strangely inaccessible under-counter storage space without damaging the room's appearance had dominated his thoughts for several days.

His footsteps echoed as he strode between the rows of pews, across the transept, and up three steps past the altar. A right turn after the choir stalls brought him to the sacristy.

"Good morning, Mrs. Morrow," he said while easing his satchel of tools onto the large leather-covered table dominating the centre of the room. "Sorry I'm late."

Elizabeth Morrow, the diminutive sacristan, smiled as she slammed the door to the vault built into a corner.

"Not a problem, Jim, and you can't be more than five minutes late." She paused, staring at a woodcut of Christ's crucifixion hanging above the door Jim entered by. "We're short of communion wine, so I'm off to fetch some. Reverend Leslie will be in her office if you need anything."

"I'll be okay. Should I lock up when I'm finished?"

Elizabeth glanced at the cabinet where Jim would be working. "I'll be back before you're done."

8

Jim removed tools from his bag as she walked away. Elizabeth had given him another opportunity to venture from home and apply his woodworking skills now he was old, alone, and at loose ends. These jobs provided meaning to his solitary life.

He crouched in front of the cabinet and assessed the problem. The solid oak countertop sat atop an elaborate pine base with inlaid panels. It was stained the dark colour often used for oak. He scribed a large rectangle on the framing and prepared to cut the opening for the new cupboard. He'd use the extracted panel to fabricate doors.

When Elizabeth returned forty-five minutes later, Jim knelt with his back toward her and his forehead against the edge of the countertop. He was staring mesmerized by his discovery when he heard the sound of the wine bottles she'd purchased clattering onto the table. His legs felt weak, and he wasn't sure he could stand.

"Are you okay?" she asked as he leaned heavily on the counter while struggling to his feet. "Should I call for help?"

He shook himself to dispel the unwelcome image that sucked the life from him. "I had a shock, but I'll recover in a minute."

He pointed, with a shaking finger, at a small bundle in the space he'd exposed. Elizabeth reached toward it, but Jim grasped her arm.

"Please," he whispered. "Fetch Reverend Leslie."

Elizabeth stared with her mouth open, then turned and rushed away. Jim sagged to his knees as the bundle reeled him in.

Minutes later, Elizabeth followed the minister into the sacristy.

Reverend Leslie glanced into the opening. "Oh, no! Can it be?" Jim watched as she reached toward the bundle but hesitated before touching it. "I should phone Chief DeWolfe."

"The police? Why would you call the police?" Elizabeth asked.

"Jim knows, don't you, Jim?" Mrs. Leslie replied.

He nodded, knowing why she must call the police, and why, in this odd community, she expected to talk to the chief, not the duty constable.

The minister crouched beside Jim. "Do you want to leave?"

He stood, twisting to face the others. "I should stay with the child."

"Child! What child? What *are* you talking about?" the sacristan demanded, her voice shrill and her eyes darting.

Reverend Leslie strode to the door. "The bundle might contain a baby's remains. That's why I must call the chief."

9

She left Jim standing by the cabinet. Elizabeth started to follow her, stopped and returned to stand with Jim.

Minutes later, Reverend Leslie reappeared, clutching her cell phone. "Chief DeWolfe says we should have a closer look without disturbing anything." She passed the phone to Elizabeth and leaned into the cabinet.

Elizabeth emitted a strangled wail, dropped the phone, and bolted.

Ms. Leslie retrieved it.

"No sign of bloodstains, just yellowed linen that appears old. It's the right size and shape for an infant." A few seconds later, she added, "We'll wait for him."

After ending the call, she turned to Jim. "The chief's sending over the new detective. Wait here while I check on Elizabeth. We're not to touch anything."

Chapter Two

By eleven that morning, Detective Goodyear had resolved the remaining issues on all but one of the open files the chief had given him. He was considering an early lunch when Chief DeWolfe's bulky frame blocked his office doorway.

The chief was a large man in his mid-fifties with closely cropped grey hair. The ruddy colour of his sun-burnished face attested to his interest in the great outdoors. "Reverend Leslie called from St. George's Church. She's discovered what appear to be human remains."

"A homeless person's decaying body, perhaps, or an ancient skeleton?"

"Not a tramp. Possibly a child's body, but nothing is clear. I told her you'd investigate."

Thoughts of lunch evaporated as Simon contemplated a case he could manage from the outset. He gathered the tools of his trade and headed for the door.

Ten minutes later, Reverend Leslie, a tall thin woman dressed in the austere black garb favoured by Anglican clergy, met Simon inside the main doors of St. George's Anglican Church. "Thank you for coming so quickly. I'm Vivian Leslie. Our discovery is this way."

She turned and marched toward the small room where Jim Ellis waited.

Mrs. Leslie strode into the sacristy. "Jim, this is Detective Simon Goodyear. Detective Goodyear, Jim Ellis, a member of our congregation. He was constructing the cupboard behind him when he discovered the bundle. It's exactly where we found it. We've disturbed nothing."

Simon surveyed the room, his eyes resting finally on four one-and-a-half litre bottles of Andres Fine Canadian Sherry sitting in mesh bags on the table dominating the small space. Three were upright; one was horizontal. "Has anyone else been here since you made the discovery?"

Reverend Leslie also focused on the wine bottles. "Mrs. Elizabeth Morrow, our sacristan," she replied before walking over to the cabinet. "The discovery made her ill. She's recuperating next door in the parish office. Nicole Adams, our office manager, is with her."

Simon nodded. "I'll ask you and Mr. Ellis to leave me to assess the situation. If it is indeed a body, I will call the medical officer and check with my office. I'll join you as soon as I can to hear your stories."

After they left, Simon conducted an initial inspection of the potential crime scene. The large, red-leather-covered table with eight mismatched chairs occupied most of the floor space in a square room, approximately five metres on each side. Three doors with inlaid panels led to other areas of the church. Matching doors for various closets, cupboards, and drawers occupied every other centimetre of wall space.

The room was dark and foreboding because everything except the ceiling and a white porcelain sink was stained a dark brown colour. Light entered through one large window with diamond-shaped panes in the wall opposite the door he entered by, and a smaller one over the cabinet Mrs. Leslie had drawn his attention to. Three dimly glowing ceiling lights provided inadequate illumination.

He knelt to inspect the bundle. It was cylindrical, sixty centimetres in length, and approximately fifteen centimetres in diameter. Simon didn't want to disturb the body, if indeed that's what they had, but he had to determine if they'd discovered human remains. He used his penknife to separate enough cloth to observe discoloured skin and a few wispy hairs on a human head.

He turned his attention to the wooden cabinet. The solidly built structure was approximately two metres long, seventy centimetres deep and one metre high, and covered by a five-centimetre-thick countertop. The freshly cut opening was rectangular, one and a half metres wide and seventy centimetres high. Two saws and the excised section of the cabinet's front face were propped against a nearby wall.

The otherwise empty under-counter space contained the bundle and sawdust from the cutting operation. The floor was the room's bare sub-floor, and the back wall, the inner face of the church's concrete exterior.

Simon detected no odour indicating decay, only a faint suggestion of pine trees.

His initial survey completed, he took numerous photos, reported to the station, and requested the presence of the medical officer. Simon returned to his car for plastic sheeting to isolate the cabinet and yellow police tape to seal the room.

Dr. Pike arrived thirty minutes later. Simon provided a summary of his observations, and Dr. Pike began his investigation. Simon was free to interview the trio involved in the discovery.

He paused in the doorway to Reverend Leslie's parish hall office. The Spartan cell was nothing like the elaborate church. Its cream-coloured walls contained a desk and three chairs. A large wooden cross adorned the wall behind the desk. "Good time for my questions?" he asked.

Vivian Leslie nodded. "I've sent Elizabeth home because she still felt queasy, but Jim and I are here. We can stay as long as necessary."

Simon wasn't pleased to learn a witness had disappeared but decided not to complain. "You could start by explaining the sacristy's purpose, and why Mr. Ellis was opening the space. I'm not a churchgoer; you may have to cover obvious things."

Reverend Leslie fingered the pewter cross hanging from a chain around her neck.

"We call it the sacristy, or sometimes the vestry, and it's used to organize everything we need for services. The clergy use it for robing, and Mrs. Morrow uses it for preparing the wine, wafers and various vessels we use. She's our sacristan, a member of the congregation who's responsible for ensuring we have what we need to conduct services."

She stopped and took a deep breath. "We generally keep it locked, but the clergy, including our lay minister and several others, have access, so it's not secure. And Mrs. Morrow has a key. The wine and our valuables are stored more safely in the vault."

"Thank you," Simon replied. "Another time, someone could perhaps give me a tour and explain how everything works. But right now, I must focus on your discovery. So, the next question, why was Mr. Ellis opening the under-counter space?"

"Three months ago, the fire marshal insisted we install a ramp for handicapped people between the floors of our parish hall. We chose to install the ramp and an elevator. We lost a meeting room used for study sessions, counting the offering after services, and various other things. We now use the sacristy for those functions."

13

Reverend Leslie stopped while she drew another breath. Simon wondered if long explanations always dominated her conversations. He smiled, thinking sermonizing might be a hazard of her trade, but said nothing to interrupt her delivery.

"This means Mrs. Morrow cannot leave the trays we use for services on the sacristy table, so we needed another place to put them. The vault is not appropriate. It's nearly full, and the door is narrow. When someone suggested using wasted space under the counter, Parish Council gave us the go ahead. We asked Mr. Ellis to create a cupboard with shelves."

"You couldn't leave the trays on the counter?"

"The plate is valuable, and many parishioners use the room. We needed a safe place to lock everything away."

Simon glanced up from his notebook. "What happened this morning?"

"Elizabeth admitted Jim to the sacristy, and he began work. He cut a rectangular opening preserving the section he removed to make doors that would fit in without altering the appearance. We would buy hinges and a locking latch for the doors giving us a secure storage location."

Simon studied the drawings he'd made. His picture of the scene unfolding that morning was beginning to make sense. "So, you hired Mr. Ellis?"

"He's a member of the congregation with skills in this area. He volunteered his time."

"And when he removed the front panel, he discovered the body."

"The space was empty except for the bundle of cloth. He must have realized what he'd discovered and sent Elizabeth to fetch me."

"And when you arrived?"

The minister generated a steeple-like shape by putting her hands together with fingertips touching. "I saw Jim kneeling in a state of obvious distress."

"Like he was praying?"

"Perhaps, or a state of contemplation. He's not devout. Mostly, I think, he was dreading what we might discover."

"What happened next?" Simon asked, hoping to avoid a diversion into theology.

"I knelt down and inspected Jim's bundle without touching it. Then I left to call Chief DeWolfe."

"And Mr. Ellis and Mrs. Morrow, what did they do?"

14

"Jim stood by the opening like he was guarding the body, making sure no one disturbed it. Elizabeth came and fetched me as I already said and waited with Jim while I phoned the chief. When I inspected the bundle, she had to leave."

"As far as you know, neither of them handled it."

"That's correct, but you should ask Jim."

Simon paused, gazing toward the door. "He's next on my agenda, but one last thing before I talk to Mr. Ellis. It looks like the cabinet was part of the original church construction."

"Correct."

"How old is the church?"

"It was built in the final years of the nineteenth century. If you want details, you should talk to John Harvey. He's our resident historian."

"Thank you. If you'll give me his number, I'll contact him. But first, I should talk to Mr. Ellis."

"You'll find him in the columbarium off the far side of the transept. His wife's ashes are there, and I suspect he's gone to tell her about this morning's adventure."

Chapter Three

Simon stopped in the sacristy doorway before locating Mr. Ellis. From one of the chairs around the sacristy table, Dr. Pike, the medical examiner, stared through the diamond-shaped panes of the larger window. The baby was gone.

"What can you tell me?" Simon asked Dr. Pike when he looked around. His placid, disinterested expression surprised Simon.

"Not a great deal. Constable Kerry collected the body for transfer to the pathologists in Halifax. I'm surprised you didn't see him."

Simon shrugged his shoulders as he glanced toward the nave. "Just missed him, I guess. You must have some information for me?"

"The deceased is female, not stillborn, weeks old when she died many years ago. I'm not qualified to estimate when."

"Is that it? Can't you tell me her race, birthmarks or physical deformities?"

Dr. Pike ignored Simon's questions. "One other thing. She was embalmed."

Embalming caught Simon's attention. It suggested something official, not the hurried disposal of a dead child. "You mean like a mummy? Or treatment you might associate with a funeral home?"

"Mummification, but you'll need the expert's opinion. A country doctor seldom encounters anything like this. The body appears well preserved."

"And you cannot tell me how she died?"

"No sign of external trauma. For anything else, you'll need the pathologist's enlightened word."

16

"When might that be?" Simon asked while resolutely staring at his notebook with pencil poised. Dr. Pike must have observed more than he acknowledged. The office scuttlebutt indicated the grey-haired and somewhat corpulent Dr. Pike was a gruff, taciturn old Scot. He was certainly living up to his reputation and giving nothing away.

"A week or two. It's not a routine case."

"You can't tell me anything else?"

Dr. Pike shook his head. "Afraid not. I have a minimal role in cases like this. I determined the remains are human. After that, we rely on the experts."

"Thank you, Dr. Pike," Simon said, looking up from his notes. "Some reason you're still here?"

"Thought I should welcome our new detective."

A brief smile flashed across Simon's face. Friendliness didn't fit Dr. Pike's reputation. "I appreciate it."

Simon walked away thinking additional information would have been more useful than friendly gestures.

As Vivian Leslie predicted, Simon found Jim Ellis in the columbarium. He sat slumped in an armchair staring at flickering votive candles on the terraced stand dominating the centre of the room. The quivering candle flames generated an ethereal appearance. Simon took another chair and waited. His gaze wandered around the room. Rows of niches containing the ashes of deceased congregation members lined the walls. A few minutes after Simon arrived, Jim emerged from his reverie.

"I was communing with Barbara. We never had children. Now, forty years later, this happens and I wonder about our choice." He shook his head. "Sorry, please forgive the mental meanderings of a doddering old fool. You have some questions?"

Mr. Ellis's pained expression suggested he was more traumatized than Reverend Leslie implied. He might have preferred a longer recovery time, but Simon had an investigation to conduct. "I need to understand this morning's events."

"Go ahead, ask your questions."

"Describe the project to open the cabinet."

"From the beginning?"

"From the first time it was mentioned."

Jim leaned forward. His expression softened as he gathered his thoughts.

17

"One week ago. Reverend Leslie and Mrs. Morrow approached me last Monday when I was fixing a broken kneeler and asked me to investigate the vestry cabinet. They explained what they wanted, and I suggested I should first determine if it was empty space. Then, I'd cut an opening like I did this afternoon."

"So, this started one week ago."

"It did for me. I located the space underneath the cabinet. The sink pipes dropped into the basement as I expected, and nothing appeared routed through the cabinet. To be sure, I bored a small hole into the cabinet from underneath the sink."

Simon consulted a sketch he'd made in his notebook. "That explains the hole I saw."

"I didn't see the bundle when I shined a light in the hole. But I saw nothing preventing me from installing Mrs. Morrow's shelves."

"Did you detect any odour?" Simon asked.

"Just a woody smell from cutting the hole."

"No indication of decay, or chemicals like formaldehyde?" Simon lacked knowledge of the chemicals used in embalming. He wrote embalming chemicals in his notebook and circled the words.

Jim shook his head. "No."

"What happened next?"

"I came in this morning to cut the opening. When I removed the central section, I noticed the bundle."

At this point, Jim's tense but controlled composure evaporated.

Simon watched tears well in his eyes. "Are you okay? We could resume this conversation later."

"Will be in a second. It's obvious the baby's been dead for some time, but the idea of jabbing it with the handsaw I used to cut the corners..." Jim dabbed his eyes and took a few deep breaths. "Please, continue."

"If you're sure. What did you do after you discovered the bundle?"

"Nothing until Mrs. Morrow returned. I knelt there saying a prayer for the little one."

"What made you suspect the bundle contained a baby?"

"I grew up in East Chester in the 1950s. Everyone knew about the butter box babies. Family friends discovered one of them, and I heard the stories. Wrapping the dead babies and disposing of them was ingrained in my mind. The bundle brought back those memories."

Simon gazed at Jim, head cocked to one side. "I'm sorry; I don't understand what you're talking about?"

18

"That's right. You're from away and wouldn't be familiar with the Ideal Maternity Home. Its operators became infamous for killing and disposing of imperfect, unwanted babies, and selling the healthy ones for big money in the Boston States. There's a book about it. They killed the unwanted babies by starving them. Then they wrapped them in linen and buried them in butter boxes, crates a local dairy used to deliver butter. It's a grisly and important part of our history. You should read about it."

After another notebook entry, Simon turned to a fresh page. His to do list was growing. Hopefully, something would bear fruit. "Thanks for the lesson. I'll look it up. So, you thought the bundle might contain the remains of a baby. What did you do?"

"Nothing. I prevented Mrs. Morrow from investigating and told her to fetch the minister. Mrs. Leslie also realized what it could be. She left to phone your people. I stood vigil touching nothing until she returned."

Simon looked up, pausing while he gathered his thoughts. "I should keep your saws to search for possible evidence clinging to the teeth. You can collect your other tools, but you won't be continuing your job until I clear the room."

Jim departed, but Simon hesitated, staring at the flickering candles. He shook his head, wondering how to explain a body in a sealed cabinet.

Chapter Four

Tuesday morning, Simon Goodyear interviewed Elizabeth Morrow at her home. The visit confirmed she remained upset by the whole experience but provided no new information. Her apprehension and unreasonable desire to be useful made her an unreliable witness, one who might add non-existent details.

Not a problem, Simon thought as he proceeded to the church, I already have two witnesses who gave me a consistent picture of Monday morning's events.

Nicole Adams, the church secretary, beckoned as he entered the nave. Her voice echoed through the empty building. "I have something for you."

The conservatively dressed, bookish-looking woman in her mid-twenties leaned against a pillar near the door to the church hall. The tone of her voice conveyed a come-hither message. Simon strolled up the centre aisle and followed her to the parish office. She reached over her desk revealing several unfastened buttons at the collar of her blouse.

She passed him a book. "Jim says you should learn our local stories."

Simon studied the cover of *Butterbox Babies* by Bette Cahill. "Mr. Ellis said I needed a Nova Scotia history lesson."

"Not just Nova Scotia, but South Shore Nova Scotia."

He laughed. "A surprising number of the townspeople grew up near here. Other Canadians say Nova Scotians have an insular perspective, but I didn't realize it extended to different parts of the province."

Nicole shrugged her shoulders. "We have the best place to live."

"I don't know about that, but Mr. Ellis grew up in East Chester. The chief and most of the police station staff are locals. I'm guessing you're part of the Adams family that's been here forever."

In the 1800s, Cornelius Barrett and four wealthy New England cronies founded Barrettsport as a summer retreat. Before the enterprising New Englanders arrived, a salt marsh isolating the townsite from the rest of the province inhibited development. Completion of the causeway in 1834 kick-started growth that produced one of Nova Scotia's most thriving communities.

One hundred and eighty years later, Adamses, Smiths, Wexlers, and Witherspoons who were descendants of four of the town's founders still dominated political and social life. No Barretts remained in Barrettsport because Cornelius only had daughters. Ettingers and Merricks, descendants of the Barrett daughters who survived to adulthood, now represented his family. The families lived northeast of town in impressive mansions on huge estates along Shore road.

Nicole stood straighter, obviously intent on defending the families' perspective. "You shouldn't hold it against us. We respect everyone's interests, not just the five families. You've only lived here a month, but that's no excuse. You should get to know us better starting next Saturday by accompanying me to our first summer garden party, one in honour of Victoria Day."

Simon glanced at the church calendar on the wall behind Nicole's desk. "But Victoria Day is two weeks away."

"That's what I said, next Saturday, the nineteenth, not this Saturday."

"Sorry. I failed to make the this-versus-next distinction, but I want to meet people. Thank you for inviting me."

"It's at the Witherspoon's starting in mid-afternoon and going into the evening, informal, outside in the garden if the weather's fine, at least until dinner time." She paused, perhaps waiting for a response. "You can get me at my apartment on Second Avenue. If it's nice, we can walk, and you needn't worry about driving your car after too many drinks." She reached out and gave his right biceps a squeeze. "I'm already looking forward to my date with a real man." She flashed a lascivious smile before abruptly changing subjects. "Any tasks for me this morning?"

Simon hesitated, taken aback by her unexpected forwardness and the suggestion they should walk. It was at least a kilometre from town to the nearest estate. "You could phone Mr. Ellis and tell him I've returned his saws. He can collect them anytime."

21

"Consider it done, and I'll expect you for coffee at ten thirty. Reverend Leslie should be here to keep you from misbehaving, and you do know there's a service today at noon."

Yeah, right, Simon thought as he retreated to the church. If anyone misbehaves it won't be me.

Her reaction shouldn't have surprised him. He was thirty-two, tall, ruggedly handsome, or so people told him, with blue eyes and short blond hair. He was fit and muscular and proud of his efforts to stay in shape. Attracting women had never been difficult, but he didn't want to repeat errors he'd made in Vancouver. He'd been a party animal with a revolving door of women entering his life, staying for a while, and leaving again. When he arrived in Barrettsport, he vowed to reform. If he wasn't careful, Ms. Adams could become the first of a new string of easy conquests.

An hour later, he'd taken photos of the sacristy emphasizing the place where they found the body, measured everything, and made a careful examination of the cabinet. He'd also taken samples of the sawdust and collected other detritus from the floor.

Simon was tidying up before Reverend Leslie and Mrs. Morrow took over the room for their pre-service activities when Jim Ellis arrived to collect his saws.

Simon pointed to the cut edge Jim produced. "Is this oak?"

"Pine. It's been stained to resemble oak," Jim replied. "The countertop is oak, but everything else in the Vestry is pine."

"But it's done in the same ornate style."

Jim ran his hand over the cabinetwork, absentmindedly caressing the lathe-turned surfaces. "They wanted the same appearance, but only used expensive materials where everyone would see them. Elsewhere, they were more frugal."

"Would they save much money using pine instead of oak if they made the inlaid panels and other finishing details?"

Jim gazed into the church. "They employed the technology of their day. There's lots of pine, so they would have saved quite a bit. They didn't cut corners in important places. The building is solid and the wood in the main church where it gets the most wear and tear is oak. Out here, and in other places where the congregation doesn't go, they used cheaper materials. Nothing wrong with that; just good, sensible, planning."

22

He said nothing while Simon collected his equipment and packaged various samples, but Jim apparently continued to ponder the construction.

"It's rather like this whole town isn't it?" he said without preamble.

Simon glanced up from his labours and paid more careful attention. "How so?"

"It has a solid foundation, at least I think it does, and the families put considerable effort into the visible side of their lives. But underneath it, plain ordinary people with plain ordinary lives dwell in plain ordinary surroundings. That's how the church works, solid foundation, impressive building, and pomp and ceremony at services. But a lot of ordinary folk keep it going. People like Mrs. Morrow, John Harvey, me, and the other volunteers."

"Interesting thought. I'll be observing Barrettsport society from the inside in a few days. I'll keep your idea in mind."

Jim paused at the door. "Been invited to the Victoria Day gala, have you? They can be gracious hosts. You should have a good time. But when it comes to the crunch, they're ordinary people like you, and me, and millions of others."

As Simon taped closed the area under the counter before joining the others for coffee, he wondered what generated Jim Ellis's jaundiced view of Barrettsport society.

Chapter Five

After midmorning coffee in the parish office, Simon ventured to Hunter's Creek to interview John Harvey.

Simon considered Jim Ellis's comments on local society as he strode to his car. Barrettsport's population was proud of its participatory democracy where citizens made important political decisions at open town meetings in the elaborate hall dominating Second Avenue. The town hall and adjacent civic offices were formal and impressive, much like the ostentatious church, but inconsistent with the realities of a modern town. This political foundation may have been solid like the fabric of the church, but a much less democratic reality lurked behind the façade.

The descendants of the original five families ran everything. The mayor and three town councillors, called selectmen in a New England tradition, had always been family members. No outsider ever held public office. Town businesses appeared stuck in the 1920s with the old family estates, and hotels, restaurants, and fancy shops catering to upper-class tourists.

The families also dominated the town's social life. It centred on the exclusive Barrettsport Yacht Club and a series of large formal parties open to the families and their carefully chosen guests.

His route took Simon along Second Avenue past the town hall and police station to the causeway joining Barrettsport to the mainland. The unincorporated commercial area between the causeway and the coastal highway was known as Upper Barrettsport. A right turn at the highway and a short drive through forested land took him to another right turn and the village at the mouth of Hunter's Creek. Along the way, he'd skirted an eighteen-hole championship golf course hidden in the forest.

The community of Hunter's Creek, population 600, was a fishing village nestled behind a spit guarding the creek's mouth. A government wharf provided the terminus for a water taxi service between Barrettsport and Hunter's Creek and protected berthing for twenty vessels, most of them inshore fishing boats. Lobster traps and other paraphernalia typical of an east coast fishing village cluttered the wharf. Hunter's Creek was only two kilometres across the harbour from Barrettsport, and less than thirty kilometres away by road, but it inhabited a different world.

John Harvey was cooking an enormous pot of chili when Simon arrived at eleven thirty. The big, burly, full-bearded man appeared comical standing over the kitchen stove wearing his wife's frilly apron.

"Lunch and dinner for the next week," John replied when Simon asked why he was making such a large batch. "If you stay for lunch, I'll be stuck with it for one less meal."

Simon laughed from his position leaning against the doorjamb. "Then, I should help you deplete the stockpile."

"Be ready in ten minutes. Meanwhile, how can I help you?"

"You presumably know Reverend Leslie found a baby girl's body tucked away in the church."

"She told me Jim Ellis discovered the body."

Simon scowled, thinking John was splitting hairs. "True. Jim found a bundle of cloth, and Reverend Leslie decided it could contain human remains before I became involved. But that's not the point. I need information on the church history to help me determine when and how the baby ended up where it did."

"In the sacristy, according to Reverend Leslie."

"In a sealed space under a counter. I need construction dates for the church and the history of renovations to the sacristy. They tell me you're the expert."

John continued to stir the chili after opening two bottles of Alexander Keith's India Pale Ale, a brand popular in Nova Scotia. He passed one to Simon. "I suppose I am. Since I retired from my career as a school teacher and moved here, I've devoted my life to local history, starting with the impressive-looking church."

Simon gazed at a sepia-toned illustration hanging on the wall behind the kitchen table. It showed a child in prayer. "So, it's not devotion to the Anglican faith?"

"My wife and I go to services, but that's not my motivation. I studied and taught history, and now I'm doing amateur historical research."

"My sources suggest your book is very professional."

"Thorough rather than professional if you ask me, and it's a work in progress. My computer has the only up-to-date copy." John stopped stirring and had a large swig of beer. "You say you're most interested in the sacristy, and the history of its furnishings?"

"Correct. I'd appreciate a broader history lesson at another time, but right now, I must focus on the sacristy and that cabinet."

John paused with head cocked to one side while tapping the wooden stirring spoon on the pot's rim. "Church construction started in 1898 and finished in 1901 although the building wasn't consecrated until the spring of 1902. Interior finishing in rooms like the sacristy, chapels, and other small rooms happened in 1901. The room has not been altered except for the sink beside the cabinet you're focused on. The original separate pedestal sink was replaced by the built-in one in the 1960s."

"I noticed that," Simon said, before sipping his beer. He should avoid chugging too many before returning to the office. "The sink cabinet doesn't seem as old as the rest."

"Or well constructed. The renovator wasn't as skilled as the workmen who built the church."

"Did your research reveal why they didn't use the space under the counter for a cupboard or drawers?"

John shook his head. "It puzzled me, but I found nothing that explained why they built it the way they did."

"And work on the cabinet? Any indication it's been altered?"

"Only the modifications to the sink, and they shouldn't impact your cabinet. The invoice describes the addition of a new cabinet with sink to the existing one."

Simon raised an eyebrow. "An actual invoice? Someone must have been a meticulous record keeper."

"They've always kept good records. It's made my job easier."

"This suggests the baby was placed there in 1901 by someone with access to the building. He must have deposited the body before the cabinet was closed in without anyone noticing her."

26

John bustled around the kitchen, grabbing bowls from an overhead cupboard and more beer from the fridge. He dumped a baguette on a cutting board. "You're thinking a workman was responsible?"

"I don't know enough to focus on anyone, but I should learn who worked on the project or had access for other reasons."

"Then, you need my book because it has a comprehensive discussion of the people involved. But first, we should eat. I hope you're okay with beer with your chili because I've opened two more, and I have French bread."

Simon tipped his first bottle and gazed at the level. It was half full. "Sounds good, and after lunch, you can lead me through your book. But what about your wife, will she be joining us?"

John laughed as he dished out the meal. "Visiting relatives in Ontario. If she were here, I would never make a week's worth of chili at one time."

After lunch, the search for someone with access to the sealed cabinet beckoned. And he had another problem niggling at his subconscious. John Harvey's bonhomie appeared forced. He and Jim Ellis were friendly and helpful. Their curiosity may have been just that, curiosity, but Simon couldn't shake the feeling they were too interested in his investigation.

Chapter Six

Barrettsport's police station presented a bright modern reception area to the public, but inside, the facility was dingy, cramped and cluttered. It may have been adequate for its task when the new reception area was constructed several decades earlier, but modern policing demanded more officers and space for computers and other modern equipment. Space they didn't have. Plans for a major rebuild had languished for years with no indication of impending action.

Simon wound his way around the various desks and workstations to his office in a corner of the single storey building. Before shedding his jacket, he opened John Harvey's email.

As he read John's history of St. George's Anglican Church, he discovered an enormous compilation of information rather than a readable book. From Simon's perspective, it was perfect, providing a wealth of data on people involved in building the church. He downloaded the file and printed the material on potential actors in the drama unfolding in 1901. The stack of printout would cover his office walls. Before leaving for the night, he ordered the largest whiteboard he could find in online catalogues. It would provide a place to display the information he collected.

That evening, as Simon strolled from the police station to the pub just outside the town boundary, he revisited the question of social opportunities in his new home. The twenty-minute walk gave him time to consider his options. His previous life in Vancouver had become intolerable. Escape from the hectic socializing that contributed to his mental and physical breakdown to a simpler life in a rural setting became his ambition. The small-town boy coveted a return to his rural roots.

28

Had his move to Barrettsport been too great a quantum shift? The peculiar and staunchly independent town's dynamic might not produce the life he sought. The town's three formal restaurants appeared on various surveys of the country's best restaurants. But it didn't sport a single pizza place, pub, or family restaurant, not even a Tim Hortons Donut Shop. Could Barrettsport, population four thousand, be the largest Canadian community without a Tim Hortons?

The lack of informal eateries necessitated this evening's walk. Regular eating establishments and the grocery stores, pharmacies, home centres, and other businesses of everyday living were located off the peninsula.

He enjoyed walking to the pub several nights a week for his solitary meals, but what would he do when he contemplated dating? What activities, for instance, could he suggest to Nicole Adams, the first young woman who'd behaved the slightest bit flirtatiously? He didn't relish inviting her to dinner at a pretentious five-star restaurant, and the only bar was the Victorian-era relic in the Traveller's Inn. There was a dearth of options between these mausoleums of the privileged classes and the pub hunkered down like a delinquent teenager just outside the town limits.

The Causeway Pub was decent enough, but a tavern with karaoke nights didn't seem like quite the place for a member of the Adams family. Then again, he thought as a blast of country music assailed his senses, what did he know about Nicole? She might relish a break from the family mould, and the Causeway Pub wasn't a stripper bar or anything like that.

Wednesday, Simon resumed his search of provincial and municipal records for information on the lives of people associated with church construction. He focused on birth records for 1900 and 1901 and spent the day determining whether those babies lived past infancy. He found no discrepancies.

A Thursday morning call from John Harvey offered respite from his ongoing excavation of ancient history. John came right to the point.

"I'll be at the church this morning. It might be our opportunity for the promised tour."

"Perfect. What time suits you?" Simon asked.

"I'm leaving now. How about nine thirty?"

"See you then."

John met Simon as he walked into the church thirty minutes later. "You look like I must when the quantity of research material becomes

29

too massive to comprehend. You should step back and contemplate something else."

"That's for certain," Nicole Adams added as she turned from rearranging leaflets at a table near the door. "I'm sure I could invent distraction-generating activities. Join us for coffee after your tour, and we can dream up something suitable." She strutted away with the exaggerated walk of a runway model.

Simon noticed the evolution of her appearance. She wore dressier shoes, her skirt was shorter and tighter, and her short-sleeved top had a V-neck showing a little cleavage.

John turned and led Simon back into the church's entranceway. "What in goodness name has gotten into Miss Nicole?"

"A little old-fashioned flirting," Simon replied, following behind.

John shook his head without commenting before pausing in the doorway. "This church's cruciform shape is generally seen in cathedrals. A cruciform layout with high vaulted ceilings is less common for parish churches, but not unknown. Undoubtedly, the wealthy citizens who commissioned this building sought a cathedral in miniature."

He stepped outside and gazed at the façade while making a magnanimous sweep with his arms. "When we approach the building, we see an imposing set of wooden doors below a stained-glass window that gives the impression it stretches to heaven. The architects wanted to emphasize height, so the doors are tall and the window much taller than it is wide."

Simon stepped past John and glanced with head cocked at the street. "I noticed the church isn't lined up with Second Avenue."

"A church should be aligned in a west-to-east direction with these main doors, formally called the Great West Doors, on the western end."

"And presumably this street doesn't quite line up in a north-south direction."

"Exactly, but most builders aren't as careful, and sometimes they basically ignored the rule. The Great West Doors of the Anglican Cathedral in Halifax, for example, are on its eastern end."

"So, it's completely backwards."

John chuckled before stepping back into the church but offered no comment on the perfidy of the Halifax cathedral's designers. "Inside these massive doors, we enter the narthex. It invites you onward into the nave, the area where the congregation sits for services. The nave is narrow and high-ceilinged. It receives its light from the stained-glass window we just inspected and the smaller ones along the side galleries.

On a bright day, these windows give an impressive picture of the church's majesty."

He strode toward the eastern end and stopped before three broad steps and a raised lectern. "We're standing in the transept, the horizontal bar of the Christian cross mimicked by the building's design. Doors on the left lead to the church's garden, those on the right, the parish hall. Generally, services are conducted from the pulpit in the transept. If we continue, we enter the chancel with the choir stalls and the organ console. St. Vincent's chapel's behind the right-hand choir stalls and the columbarium behind the left-hand ones."

"Monday afternoon, I found Mr. Ellis in the columbarium, but I wasn't aware of the chapel."

John ignored Simon's interjection. "Next, we pass the sacristy and similar room on the left where the choir practices. Finally, we approach the sanctuary and the high altar."

Simon stopped and pointed toward the transept. "You said services are conducted back there."

"This altar is used for certain important functions. Reverend Leslie can give you the details if you're interested. My focus is on the building, not the ceremony."

Simon looked back toward the window above the entrance. "It's impressive, especially the four large stained-glass windows. I hadn't noticed the ones in the transept until this morning. And this one is quite something," he added, turning as he gazed at the window over the high altar.

"They are beautiful. That's the formal public part of the church. If you follow me, I'll show you the hidden part most of us never see."

John entered a door across the chancel from the sacristy door Simon was already familiar with. He poked his head into the room. "This is the servers' vestry. It's used by choir members and servers." He pressed on. "This door enters a narrow passageway called the ambulatory. It circles behind the high altar to the sacristy."

"I noticed that passageway on Monday but didn't investigate."

John pointed to various features as they walked behind the high altar, stopping finally at a vertical ladder hidden behind a tall, narrow door.

"This ladder leads to empty space above the sacristy and St. Vincent's chapel. It has access to the organ pipes and the rope for the church bell."

Simon stared at the dark confines of the chimney-like closet containing the ladder. He didn't relish the idea of squeezing into the

31

confined space but his primary task demanded a look at the room immediately above the sacristy. If he saw anything interesting, he would return to conduct a more thorough investigation.

Simon turned and addressed John. "Do we have access?"

John laughed. "I'll wait here because the ladder's not for someone as old and unfit as me. But you're welcome to visit provided you don't ring the bell."

Simon rested his hand on a ladder rung, smiled at the unexpected hint of informality in a proper, scholarly tour, and began his ascent. "Of course not."

After John explained the mechanism for releasing the upper room's trap door, Simon felt for the deadbolt. When he pushed open the hatch, light filled the closet and everything became less intimidating.

Concrete buttresses of the church structure dominated the space he encountered. Two of the interior walls contained the workings for the organ pipes. He found a narrow staircase leading to the gallery around the church tower in one corner.

Simon conducted a quick inspection of the empty room before climbing the staircase and peering at the harbour through the openings in the tower.

He descended to ground level. "The view's not as spectacular as I expected. And I didn't find the pull rope for the church bell."

"The tower is shorter than many, so we don't get the eye-popping views. And modern buildings like the big apartments tower over this old church."

John opened the sacristy door. "It's coffee time. I must speak to Reverend Leslie, so you and Miss Nicole can return to your old-fashioned flirting."

As they proceeded to the church hall via the sacristy and the little chapel Simon hadn't seen before, he considered his private tour. It had been an interesting interlude providing background information that might prove useful, but he didn't think he'd learned anything critical to his case.

Chapter Seven

John Harvey disappeared into Reverend Leslie's office to conduct the business that brought him to the church. Nicole was left to entertain Simon. "Are you as overwhelmed by information overload as Mr. Harvey suggested?"

"The problem's lack of insight, not volume of data."

She pushed the coffee tray aside and perched coquettishly on the table. "So, you do need a break."

"I suppose, but I'll get one on the weekend. I needn't work twenty-four seven on a century-old problem."

"Then perhaps we could join forces on Saturday."

Simon raised a quizzical eyebrow. "Are you asking me out on another date?"

"Not a real date, but I'm going shopping. If you need anything in the big city, we could travel together, have lunch in Halifax, and make a day of it. And I wouldn't have to borrow Daddy's car."

Simon chuckled. It sounded like an oddball date to him. "And dine together when we return?"

She smiled. "That would be nice."

"Then I should make a dinner reservation. Any preference?"

She jumped down from the table and began gathering the coffee cups. "Why don't we wing it, find something when we get back. We won't have deadlines to worry about."

Simon shook his head, thinking her banter was too pat. But what the hell, he had no weekend commitments. "Saturday morning. Is nine too early?"

"Nine would be great. Thank you, I'm looking forward to it already." Nicole looked up and turned toward the sacristan as she arrived in the doorway. "Oh, Mrs. Morrow. Reverend Leslie is talking to Mr. Harvey, but she should be available shortly. Can I offer you tea or coffee?"

"No thank you, Nicole, and I don't need to see her. I'll proceed with setting up for the noontime service if Detective Goodyear has no more questions for me."

The interruption gave Simon a chance to watch Nicole. She seemed years younger and much less conservative than she had two days earlier. A ponytail cascading down her back had replaced the tight bundle pinned behind her head. The outdated glasses were gone, presumably replaced by contact lenses. Her clothes were less formal, still reasonable attire for someone in an office environment but friendlier, and well, younger. He wondered if the congregation might find her new look too informal.

Friday morning at ten thirty, Simon found himself an empty table at the Tim Hortons in Upper Barrettsport between the Causeway Pub and the highway. He placed his plain cake donut on the napkin he'd spread on the table and prised the lid off his plastic Tim Hortons coffee-to-go cup. Richard Merrick, Barrettsport's robust but grey-haired mayor, sauntered through the crowd waving to everyone and sat opposite him.

"Mind if I join you?" Mayor Merrick asked as he stirred sugar into coffee in a large ceramic mug.

Simon glanced up surprised by the mayor's appearance at his table in the coffee shop just outside the town limits. He wondered what it might mean.

"Never liked plastic coffee mugs," the mayor added, pointing his stirring stick at Simon's. "And those paper ones..." He shook his head while rolling his eyes.

"So, you don't participate in the 'roll up the rim to win' contests," Simon replied. His surprise turned to admiration as he realized how the mayor, a consummate politician, managed to use a simple comment about mugs to make the meeting seem coincidental.

Mayor Merrick must have picked up on Simon's initial reaction. "I suppose you're wondering why I'm here."

"Yes, sir, I am rather."

"Chief DeWolfe suggested I might find you here, and I did want a quick word. You know, take the opportunity to become better

34

acquainted with our new detective." He spread his arms in a magnanimous gesture. "I jumped at the chance and here I am."

"Well, sir, it's unlike anything I experienced out west."

"We do things differently in our little town. And Simon, you can start by calling me Richard."

After numerous seemingly meaningless questions about Simon's new home, the mayor approached the problem behind this unusual meeting. "And how is the new case going?"

Simon paused, wondering how he should respond. Was Mayor Merrick making idle conversation, or was he pumping Simon for information? And if he wanted inside information, why didn't he ask Chief DeWolfe? Determining what to say would become the chief's problem.

Simon took a deep breath. "We have the body of a baby girl, but not stillborn. She was discovered in a space sealed shut since church construction."

"Not someone who died more recently, say in the last fifty years?"

Simon watched the mayor's eyes, hoping his expression would give something away. But the skilled politician gave nothing away. "The autopsy and forensics reports should clarify the situation, but it appears she died a hundred years ago."

"Good. I was worried you were describing a more recent event."

"Good?" Simon asked, thinking the mayor had finally let something slip. "I don't see what's good about it. We need to discover her identity and whatever we can about her fate."

"I'm sorry. I didn't mean to sound cavalier. I agree we need to identify her and determine what happened, but whoever was responsible will have long since passed away. You won't be investigating crimes involving living people."

Simon shrugged his shoulders and watched carefully as the mayor moved on to other subjects before taking his leave. Had he tensed up when he broached the subject of Simon's case? Was he concerned about the inappropriateness of his questions? If so, why did he pose them? And why was he relieved when Simon described a one-hundred-year-old crime? Because that meant political ramifications were less likely? Or was something else worrying him?

Several times during Simon's short tenure in Barrettsport, Chief DeWolfe had complained about the way the mayor and council meddled in police affairs. They appeared obsessed with damage control to minimize the impact of anything reflecting badly on the town. And why did Mayor Merrick relax when he learned it was an old problem? In this history obsessed town, wouldn't he worry as much about a one-hundred-year-old event as a fifty-year-old one?

Simon strode back to the office wondering if there was more to this incident than the 'families' annoying habit of controlling everything and everyone. Probably not, he decided as he walked into the station, but the doubts remained. Did the mayor know something that occurred during his lifetime? Something he was withholding from the police? Was this Simon's first exposure to the family patriarchs' manipulation of civic affairs?

Chapter Eight

At five minutes before nine Saturday morning, Simon pulled up at Nicole's Second Avenue address. It didn't seem like the sort of date where one arrived fashionably late.

Nicole came tripping down the stairs from her second-floor apartment above a shop before Simon opened the street-level door. She appeared even younger than she did Thursday morning, sporting sandals with considerable heel, bright red shorts barely substantial enough to be decent, and a midriff-baring frilly white blouse with half the buttons undone. Her ash-blond hair done in pigtails high up on each side of her head seemed paler than it did previously. She looked hardly more than a teenager, perhaps a university undergraduate, but not someone in her late twenties.

Nicole pirouetted on the sidewalk ending with an exaggerated gesture that suggested she'd taken ballet lessons during her youth. "You like my transformation from church secretary into fun-loving party girl?"

"You look smashing, but we're going shopping, not partying."

"But I couldn't resist the opportunity to let my hair down. I hope you don't mind."

"Your hair's more up than down."

She shook her head, setting her tails in motion. "Do you like them?"

"Kind of cute, but not appropriate for one of Barrettsport's formal restaurants."

"We should go somewhere less formal, but we needn't worry until evening." She glanced at Simon, also casually dressed in loafers, jeans, and a golf shirt. "Anyway, you're no better dressed than me."

37

After an early lunch at a Boston Pizza, they hit the large industrial park with big-box stores on the edge of Halifax. Simon found his odd 'date' entertaining and informative because she nattered about her life growing up in Barrettsport.

Nicole clapped her hands as they entered Lee Valley Tools, their final stop before heading home, and the first one for Simon's benefit. "Neat! I love these stores where you tell a clerk what you want, and he retrieves it from the storeroom. When I was little, every Barrettsport store worked this way. Now they've converted to self-serve like everywhere else."

"Shoe stores. I remember when shoe stores were like this, but that's not what brought me here. It has unusual toys for inquisitive young minds."

"Oh. Why does that interest you?" Nicole asked.

Simon showed her a three-dimensional wooden puzzle that assembled into a dinosaur. "It's for my nephew. He was upset when he learned I was moving so far away. He's into puzzles and dinosaurs, so I thought I should send him one for his birthday."

Nicole said nothing until they were homeward bound in Simon's car.

"I thought you were like a cowbird's egg, left for someone else to raise."

"Nothing like that. Two normal parents, rather older than most when they started a family, and an older brother. My parents have died, but my brother's married, living in Prince George in northern British Columbia."

"And they have a little boy. You didn't tell me his name."

Simon glanced over as she leaned toward him. She was either really interested or doing a damn good job of faking it. "Donnie, he's six, and he has a little sister, Hannah, but she's too young for dinosaurs or anything else the slightest bit interesting."

"Aren't you the man of surprises. Everyone thinks you're completely alone."

"I don't know why. And what about you, you're also pretty full of surprises."

"Why's that?"

"Rich girl like you shopping at Walmart and the other discount stores. Can't help wondering why."

Nicole burst out laughing as Simon manoeuvred around a car that pulled onto the shoulder without warning. "You have any idea how little money a church secretary makes?"

38

"Obviously not as much as Bill Gates, but wouldn't your folks help?"

"They think I should live in the family home until I marry. When I rented my own place, I was left to my own resources. This is all I can afford."

"Yeah, right. I'm not convinced I'll see you at Saturday's garden party in a dress you bought at Frenchie's Used Clothing."

"Have you been to a Frenchie's? Sometimes you find the most amazing things. But seriously, my folks will spring for a new party outfit but not everyday stuff. Today I'm wearing clothes I found in the bargain bins at Walmart, and that's closer to my world than designer dresses."

"What should we do for dinner?" Simon asked an hour later as he helped her move her purchases into her apartment. It was almost seven, and he was getting downright hungry. They'd had an early lunch and only one short break for coffee. Nicole had a piece of pie and ice cream with her mid-afternoon coffee, but Simon only had coffee. He now regretted his forbearance. "Should we change and find a table at a restaurant?"

"Let's go to the Causeway Pub!"

Simon shouldn't have been surprised; Nicole spent the whole day escaping from her normal routine. She hadn't pretended otherwise, thanking Simon several times for his contributions to her flight of fancy.

"We're late for getting food service before whatever noisy country music band they've hired starts up. You sure you want to go there?"

"I've never been to a pub with a cowboy band. Wouldn't miss it for the world. I won't even need to change, just grab my jacket and go."

Simon smiled. Nicole's flight of fancy was still in full swing. There was clearly no stopping her.

They found a table far from the stage and had their orders in before the musicians hit their first notes. It wasn't too noisy, just a young woman singer with three backing musicians playing folk-rock music from thirty years earlier. A pleasant change from the down-home country music the Causeway Pub favoured. The pub owner had announced a karaoke competition during the singer's break, and Nicole talked about nothing else during the first set. She was determined to participate, and Simon couldn't dissuade her.

Towards the end of the set, Nicole approached the bar and had a discussion with the bartender organizing the karaoke competition. She turned and did a war dance for Simon's benefit before disappearing into

39

the women's washroom. When she returned to their table a few minutes later, she surreptitiously passed Simon her bra.

"Keep this for me, will you?" she whispered, leaning toward him. Only one strategically placed button on her blouse was done up and her breasts were pushed upward in an unnatural way. She must have brought a second push-up bra that left them mostly exposed. She wasn't indecent; Simon had seen many women in designer gowns that exposed just as much cleavage. Hardly a modest look, but he had to admit, perfect for a karaoke competition. As she strutted to join the motley array of performers queued up for the competition, Simon realized she'd planned the entire caper.

The first few contestants sang country and western songs, mostly not too well, and the guy running the sound system cranked the volume to give them a helping hand. When Nicole walked to the mike and cued the disc jockey, he increased the volume of her intro to quiet the crowd, then dropped it to a whisper. She sang the first line to Mary Hopkin's *Those Were the Days* with such authority the background noise dropped to nothing before she reached the refrain. With her pigtails in motion and pushed-up breasts straining to escape from her blouse, she looked like a teenage hooker on the make. She didn't fit anyone's image of a chanteuse singing a nostalgic old song, but she had the crowd in her hands. When the votes were tallied, she'd easily won the competition.

The prize, a huge German beer stein with a hinged lid, was decorated with bas-relief images of scantily clothed young maidens cavorting in a tavern. The DJ presented it to Nicole as the real musicians reclaimed the stage.

She returned to their table with her stein-full of beer, pushed her chair over next to Simon's and sighed. "That was so much fun, but I can't possibly drink all this beer."

"You should be thankful the crowd didn't insist you chug it at the bar. When the second set's done, I expect your stein to be empty."

She took one big gulp before leaning over and whispering in his ear, "You could help a little."

Nicole was subdued as they walked home hand-in-hand like teenagers on a first date.

"You've given me a great deal to consider," she said when they arrived outside her door. "I've enjoyed myself immensely, but..."

"I know, it's late and good girls don't invite guys up to their apartments on the first date." He gave her a quick kiss but didn't try to extend it because she was almost in tears. "We both need time."

She hugged him and disappeared up the stairs. He stood on the sidewalk wondering why she became so emotional.

Simon returned to his apartment wondering about Nicole and Barrettsport society. He wasn't ready for a new relationship, so thankful she hadn't invited him in. He was still recovering from traumatic events in Vancouver and keen to avoid romantic entanglements with the Barrettsport families. They fascinated him, but after Nicole described how they thought and behaved, he knew he would never fit into their society.

She'd provided him with an unexpectedly entertaining and informative day. He retired wondering how her family would react to the stein she'd promised to display among her favourite possessions.

Chapter Nine

Tuesday, May fifteenth, the medical examiner's report returned Simon's investigation to square one. It showed the baby died in the 1950s or 1960s. Several pieces of evidence pointed to a date no earlier than 1950. These included the body's condition, the embalming chemicals and processes, and the synthetic thread used to hem the cloth. Estimates for the date of death gave a 1950 to 1965 window.

The report described the baby's age at death as less than six weeks. She was a Caucasian female with no sign of mistreatment or identifiable diseases. The cause of death was most likely intentional or accidental suffocation. It gave no firm basis for a homicide investigation.

The report contained extensive details of textiles and embalming techniques that would require research, but the bottom line was clear. He needed to focus on the 1950s and '60s rather than 1900. If someone placed the body in the sealed cabinet during the more recent period, he had to discover how it was done.

"It's incumbent on us to identify the child and determine who deposited the body in the cabinet," Chief DeWolfe said when Simon reported his results.

"And how he did it," Simon added.

The chief smiled. "You probably won't figure out who until you determine how."

"So, I should continue."

"Definitely. It's even more important now we know the baby died only fifty or sixty years ago. I don't want this mystery hanging over our town."

"But we're unlikely to produce definitive evidence leading to a conviction."

"The file remains open forever if we don't identify the child. If we can identify the person responsible for disposal, we should try to build a case."

Simon gathered the evidence he'd brought into the chief's office. The chief's quest might be hopeless, but it was an interesting mystery that would keep his mind occupied until he had a more pressing case. And the latest revelations put a different spin on the conversation he'd had with Barrettsport's mayor four days earlier.

Wednesday morning, he was back in the sacristy waiting for Jim Ellis.

"So, Mr. Ellis," Simon said when Jim arrived, "Once again, I need your help."

Jim dumped his tool bag on the floor. "I haven't been messing with your crime scene."

"No one's accusing you, but we have new evidence, and I must consider the possibility someone accessed this cabinet after 1902."

"And you think I can tell?"

"Exactly."

Jim shook his head. "You need someone who's more expert than me. Don't you have specialists in the RCMP or the Halifax force?"

"They told me to consult a master carpenter or cabinet maker."

"That's definitely not me," Jim said, laughing. "I'm a rough carpenter at best."

"Then who should I consult?"

"Let me think." He gazed around the sacristy while tapping his second finger on the side of his head. "Josh Corkum is probably your best bet if you want someone nearby. He's a wooden-boat builder and the best woodworker I can think of. He lives and works in Hunter's Creek and John Harvey knows him. If you want another opinion you might ask John, but I'd say he's your man."

"Thank you. I'll contact him and see if he can assess things for me. Then I can give you an update on when you can return to work."

"Good. Mrs. Morrow keeps asking about it. I don't see the reason for panic. They've been managing for a hundred years, but she's impatient."

Simon laughed. "Let's see what Mr. Corkum says, and then maybe we can avoid Mrs. Morrow's wrath."

Half an hour later, Jim had gone to repair shelves near the front of the church. Simon was talking to Nicole while waiting for Josh Corkum.

"Have you recovered from your Sunday morning hangover?" Simon asked. Nicole had reverted to the serious woman he'd met on day one, not the wild young thing she'd evolved into by Saturday evening.

"I felt great Sunday, still revelling from Saturday's experiences. It was super, the most fun I've had in years. The problems started Monday when my parents learned about Saturday night. I may be twenty-six and a supposedly independent adult, but as far as they're concerned, I'm still their little girl."

Simon paused wondering why a twenty-six-year-old woman would be so concerned about her parent's reaction. "Do they object to you participating in karaoke competitions?"

"They objected to my get-up, and I guess it was a little much."

Simon shook his head thinking about the other contestants. Compared to some of the others, Nicole's attire and behaviour were downright demure. "It wasn't obscene or anything, just playful and a little risqué. And no disasters. Nothing like that girl's serious costume malfunction."

"An intentional one, if you ask me."

"Should we pass on this weekend's party?" Simon asked.

"Oh no! You must come. You're a hero in their eyes for keeping me out of serious trouble. It'll cause more difficulty if I don't produce you Saturday."

"Good because I'm looking forward to it, but I didn't keep you out of trouble."

"The other time I became adventurous, I was arrested, and they had to bail me out. When nothing happened on Saturday, they had to give the credit to someone, and that someone was you!"

Jim Ellis arrived eliminating Simon's opportunity to discover the indiscretion Nicole referred to. She probably wasn't prepared to tell him, anyway.

Jim stepped into the parish office with someone right behind him. "Detective Goodyear, this is Josh Corkum."

The man's appearance surprised Simon. He looked very young, no more than mid-twenties, short and slight with a full beard and longish brown hair. The beard might have contained a few wood chips. He wore work boots, blue jeans that probably needed a wash, and a plaid lumberjack's shirt. He reminded Simon of a PBS show about a young carpenter in North Carolina or some such place. The host took viewers

44

to a rustic workshop where he made things using old-fashioned hand tools. Simon couldn't remember the show's name, but he imagined Josh Corkum hosting a similar program, perhaps one with a boat-building theme.

"Thank you, Mr. Corkum," Simon said, stepping forward with his hand extended. "I appreciate your coming here at such short notice."

"No problem, and please call me Josh."

"Okay Josh, if you will come with us to the sacristy, I'll describe our problem."

After Simon explained their difficulty, Josh leaned into the cabinet with a multi-bulb LED flashlight and made a careful inspection of the internal structure. He then repeated the process going over the exterior surfaces before extending his assessment to the section Jim removed and the sink unit beside the cabinet.

"Okay, here's what I think," he said, finally standing upright after ten minutes crawling around the floor. He showed no ill effects from his exertions.

Simon held up a restraining hand. "Slowly, please while I take notes."

"First, I see no indication the front's been removed since it was installed. But if it was rebuilt in the 1950s, they would have used modern glues. I suggest you go in there with a sharp knife, scrape the excess glue into one of your evidence bags, and send it to your lab for analysis. If it contains both 1900 glue and 1950 glue, your forensics lab technicians should be able to tell."

"You seem to know about forensic labs," Simon replied.

"I plead guilty to watching those TV shows about crime labs. I'm rather addicted to them." Josh gave them a sheepish smile before continuing. "You cannot dismantle the top without removing the screws holding it to the base. You can't do that without accessing all four corners from below. The right-hand side is fixed because the cabinet and adjacent wardrobe were built together. You'd have to cut away a section to gain access, and that's not been done."

"So that leaves us with the partition between our cabinet and the sink unit," Jim suggested.

"And it looks like one of the inset panels has been detached."

"Why so?" Simon asked.

Josh pointed at the trim surrounding one of the panels. "Because those four boards don't fit together properly. Someone removed the panel and did an amateurish job reassembling it."

Simon crouched down and squeezed his head and one arm through the small opening beneath the sink. He photographed the badly aligned joint. "But it's one small panel tucked in behind the sink. Does it give someone the access he would need?"

"Not unless he took the sink unit apart. It's newer and less carefully made, and apparently joined to your cabinet with a few screws and no glue. It could be removed without causing any damage and reinstalled after the deed was done."

"Couldn't someone simply gain access from under the sink?" Jim asked. This inspection definitely had his attention.

"Too awkward and the framing for the sink unit would prevent it. You'd have to remove the front section."

"Hang on a minute," Simon interjected before turning to Josh. "Couldn't he make it easier for himself by removing a panel from the front of the main cabinet?"

Josh shook his head. "Damage on the front face would show, but damage under the sink is hidden. If we remove the front of the sink unit, everything should be obvious."

Simon glanced from Jim to the sink unit. "Can you do that?"

"Don't see why not."

Josh pocketed his trusty flashlight, the only tool he'd brought with him. "I have an errand to run, but I could return and give you my opinion if necessary."

"Yes, by all means. It would be best if you finished the job you've started," Simon replied.

"Does that mean you expect me to describe this in court?"

"It's unlikely to go to court, but I prefer to keep my narratives simple and straightforward. Continuity helps."

"Okay, I'll return in half an hour."

Jim began by removing the front face of the sink unit. It came apart without removing the sink. Simon timed the exercise, it took twenty minutes. He also generated a photographic record.

"He's right," Jim said, pointing. "See those four pieces of decorative moulding? They're only held in place with small nails and it's now obvious someone removed them."

Simon once again stuck his head into the confined space. "The boards on the back hold the panel in place, and these bits of trim prevent it falling forward. It's not glued or nailed."

"That's right."

When Josh returned, he smiled and nodded his head after another careful inspection of the job. He was obviously pleased Jim's efforts confirmed his original observations.

He drew Simon's attention to the critical panel by focusing his light on one corner. "Those marks show where someone slid a blade under the trim and slowly worked it loose. I can see similar marks on the adjacent panel, so I suspect he removed both of them. And no marks on the panels from the front section."

"So, he reused the pieces. He wouldn't have replaced them?"

"Not possible, first it would be difficult to match the stain perfectly, and second, mouldings made in the 1950s weren't the same as ones made in 1900."

"And the remaining panels haven't been tampered with?"

Josh shone his light from panel to panel, taking a final look at each of them. "That's my opinion, and if he hadn't done such a poor job of replacing the trim on the first panel we may never have noticed anyone tampered with them. You should photograph the marks, and you may want to have someone else look at it, but that's what I think."

"One last thing. How long would it take to remove the panels and replace them, patching everything up? You know, the whole job from beginning to end."

Josh glanced at Jim before answering. "One hour when no one entered the room."

"And how much noise would it make?"

"Not a lot, but some. Boards squeak when you pull them away, and there would also be tapping sounds."

By noon, Simon had detailed photographs of all six panels and a new perspective on the mystery of the baby in the sealed cupboard. He also had a new question to ponder. Was Jim showing the curiosity of a fellow carpenter while watching Josh's investigation, or did his interest suggest something more sinister?

47

Chapter Ten

Detective Simon Goodyear spent the rest of the week investigating the history of Barrettsport during the 1950s and 1960s rather than the end of the previous century. He focused on infants who went missing during the more recent period when vital statistics were more carefully recorded. Could a baby live for a few weeks without generating a retrievable record?

He couldn't discount the possibility of an unrecorded home birth, but he doubted such a birth occurred in a small town without someone noticing. He tapped into newspaper reports and questioned elderly residents hoping to find anyone who remembered an unregistered baby.

By Saturday afternoon and the garden party at the Witherspoon's, he was no further ahead. He'd gathered masses of information on social activities from the local newspaper but found no indication of a missing baby girl. And so far, interviews had produced nothing tangible. Perhaps he'd discover a lead at the party.

The weather was inauspicious for a garden party, cool, overcast and threatening rain. Simon arrived at Nicole's apartment at two thirty. She was elegantly dressed when she answered the door immediately after his knock. A totally different look, not the austere church secretary, not the flirtatious pigtailed school girl, but a sexy young socialite dressed to impress. The dress was an ankle length, ivory coloured, sleeveless affair with several lace panels in the top. The skirt was slit up both sides to mid-thigh.

"Greetings, Nicole, I hope I'm not too early."

"Almost perfect. Fetch yourself a glass of wine. I'll be ready momentarily." She pointed toward her small galley-style kitchen before hustling down a hallway without waiting for Simon's reply. "I'll be ready in a few minutes," she repeated.

Simon helped himself to a glass of Chardonnay and extracted the bra she'd given him for safekeeping before the karaoke competition from his pocket. He found a large teddy bear and was adorning the bear with the bra when she caught him.

"Ah, you brought back my bra! I worried we'd left it behind in the pub. Here, give it to me. Do you think I should wear it Madonna-style outside my dress?" She held the bra in front of her and waited for his response. Her frivolous attitude was in stark contrast with her designer party dress.

He looked at her and smiled. "I don't think that's today's look, and it spoils an elegant dress."

"Nice isn't it," she said doing a twirl while holding the bra at arm's length before flinging it onto one of her living room chairs. "The benefits of having rich parents. It's one of my Christmas presents, and this is the first opportunity I've had to wear it."

"Will it be warm enough? It's not very summery out there. You might want to save it for a warmer day and wear something else."

"I'll be fine, I have a wrap I can wear, and anyway, you can always hug me if I get chilly."

He laughed. Her appearance may have changed, but it hadn't affected her flirty behaviour. "Should we be going?"

"Yes, my handsome escort, lead on." She took his arm and pulled him through the door. If this continues, Simon thought as he pulled her door closed and checked it was locked, I'll be leading from behind.

Their hosts had gone all out on the extensive lawn stretching in a series of broad terraces to the shore. It sported a tennis court, a decorative garden with a maze, and a swimming pool. The tennis court was ready for action, croquet and other games were set up on the lawn, and the pool steamed in the cool air. Attendants even waited to give little kids pony rides.

The weather had not dampened the children's enthusiasm. Some rode ponies, others swam in the pool, and from the noise emanating from the garden, more frolicked unseen in the maze. A group of young adults played croquet, but most of the tables and chairs on the grounds were empty. The newly arriving guests congregated near the bar set up on an amazing multi-level complex of decks and patios.

Nicole and Simon joined the throng on the patios, and she introduced him to her parents and other members of the families.

Simon was surprised to find the scruffy Josh Corkum among the guests but less surprised to discover the professorial John Harvey. A few minutes later, he noticed a number of others, including a young school teacher, and several members of the arts community. A goodly number of outsiders attended this Barrettsport family party.

An hour after they arrived, as the skies continued to darken, Josh sat without ceremony on the broad wooden arm of Nicole's Adirondack chair. Their easy demeanour surprised Simon. They'd only shared a few words when Josh helped Simon with his investigations a few days earlier, but now they seemed like long-lost friends.

"I hope he's not giving you the grilling he gave me," Josh said to Nicole, gesturing toward Simon. "How's it going? I haven't seen you for ages."

Nicole banged her chair's other arm. "What do you mean? You saw me three days ago!"

"That didn't count. You looked so severe I couldn't say anything. You reminded me of the matrons in the convent you lived in through college."

"As you can tell," Nicole said, turning toward Simon. "Josh and I have known each other for some time, and he's no nicer to me now than he was then."

"How can you say not nice? I would have done anything for you, but you never noticed me. You were blind to anyone but Mr. Edward Beardsley."

Nicole harrumphed, eyes focused on Simon's. Josh was only centimetres away, but Nicole was making a show of ignoring him.

"You should have seen that guy," Josh added for Simon's benefit. "He was so pretentious, always Mr. Beardsley or Edward even to his fellow students."

"What do you mean? I called him Teddy Bear all the time!" Nicole interjected, unable to separate herself from the conversation.

"You were so madly in love he allowed you a few liberties, but none of us could call him Ted or Teddy."

"So, what happened to Mr. Teddy Bear?" Simon asked Nicole. "Why aren't you happily married?"

"I got fed up with waiting for his proposal. I mean we dated for three years, and during that whole time he insisted we live separately and behave with *discretion*."

"Never anything like your karaoke performance Saturday night," Josh added.

Nicole puckered her nose. "Heard about that, did you?"

"Like everyone else in town. I wish I'd been there. Maybe you should do a repeat performance this evening."

"I think not. My parents were really unhappy."

Josh sighed, but the mischievous twinkle in his eyes told the real story. He enjoyed teasing her. "Too bad, I would have enjoyed it. But we were talking about Beardsley."

"Yes, getting back to Teddy, we only became lovers toward the end of our senior year. He wouldn't even consider me going with him to graduate school. After what's now eight years, I'm not sure I want him anymore."

"What! I heard he finally proposed." Josh was undeterred by Simon's presence and either unaware of or ignoring Nicole's uneasiness.

"Hardly! About six weeks ago, he provided a status report announcing he'd received his Ph.D. and was off to another posting, something he called a post-doc. It wasn't a proposal, more of a feeler to see if I'm still interested."

"What did you tell him?"

"What's with you, Josh? This isn't a proper conversation especially with Simon here."

"I don't care what's proper or improper. What did you tell him?"

"Nothing! I haven't decided how to respond."

"Then this might be my last chance," Josh said before sliding to one knee. "Nicole, I've loved you since I first noticed you at your frosh orientation. Will you marry me?"

"Oh Josh, quit being a fool," Nicole said, getting up and stepping around him. "I'll pretend you never said that."

She blushed and had a tremor in her voice. Josh's proposal obviously impressed her more than she wanted to admit. Josh jumped up, insisting on another round of drinks. He was clearly happy as he skipped toward the bar.

Nicole slumped into her chair. "He always was a fool."

The rain started after Josh returned with a bottle of bubbly and three Champagne flutes. He insisted they toast his courage for finally expressing his love for the woman he'd loved for eight long years before he let them escape from the shower. He seemed happy he'd expressed his feelings for Nicole and content to let her consider things.

51

"That's just like Josh," Nicole concluded. "He really is sweet, much nicer than Teddy Bear Beardsley."

Josh disappeared and Nicole escorted Simon through the rooms on the main floor of the Witherspoon's elaborate mansion.

The doors dominating the centre of the façade opened into a large formal entrance foyer. Curved stairways led to second-floor galleries and the bedrooms and other private accommodations.

Two hallways led off the foyer. The left-hand one joined a dining room and two small sitting rooms facing the ocean with a large kitchen facing the street. The dining room was very formal with a table that would seat at least twelve, but the two sitting rooms were cozy and decorated with a feminine touch. The right-hand hallway led to a library, a billiards room and a study or office. These rooms had a masculine feel.

Large panelled doors between the stairways led from the foyer to a reception room stretching through to the back of the house between the dining room and the library. Nicole called it a ballroom, describing the size of the orchestra and the large number of dancers it could accommodate. On this occasion, a series of white-clothed tables for dispensing a buffet supper was located in the orchestra's corner. Tables and chairs for the dinner guests surrounded the dance floor.

During the informal buffet dinner, Nicole introduced Simon to more family members, and he soon realized how tightly knit their society was. Everyone seemed related to everyone else as many sons of one family had married daughters of another. If sons ventured outside their community in search of wives, they appeared to marry women from a small group of New England families, keeping the family gene pool rather restricted. Several men from these New England families had married into the local family circle generating a second tier of interrelated families. Powells and Campbells, who both had large houses on the peninsula, represented this group, but the one who stood out was Caroline Garrett, the daughter of Charles Wexler. The Garretts owned an ostentatious new house that made the original mansions look small.

Caroline, whose husband, investment advisor and selectman Matthew Garrett, didn't appear to be in attendance, cornered Simon when he tried to escape the mayhem and enjoy the delicacies on the dessert trays. Nicole had given Simon a factual breakdown of the interrelationships. Caroline augmented his picture with more interesting stories about the behind-the-scenes lives of many of the family members. It was a litany of alleged affairs involving several generations of the bastions of their male-dominated society.

52

When she stumbled away for another drink, Simon scribbled a few notes. Mrs. Garrett had told him a number of interesting tidbits about people in the town, including a few leads that might connect to the baby he was trying to identify. Something made her a less than happy camper, but Simon couldn't understand why she insisted on telling him these stories.

Chapter Eleven

Victoria Day Monday was a holiday, but the rain that started Saturday afternoon as Josh expressed his love for Nicole, continued unabated through Sunday and into Monday morning. With nothing to distract him, Simon focused on his investigation. He had no new leads and wasn't enthusiastic about additional research into parish activities in the middle decades of the twentieth century. But he preferred to sit in his office pondering the problem, rather than remain alone in his almost empty apartment staring at the bare walls.

The apartment also raised questions about his commitment to his new life in Barrettsport. He'd only shipped his home gym and minimal furnishings from Vancouver, trashing all the cast-offs he'd used to furnish his west coast apartment. He planned to furnish his Barrettsport apartment with new modern furniture, not yard sale junk. But he'd made no effort to implement his plan. He had three stools by the kitchen counter and his recliner chair with a wooden crate masquerading as a living room table. The rest of the open plan kitchen/dining/living area was empty space. His bedroom had a bed and another wooden crate for a bedside table, and the spare bedroom, the equipment for his home gym.

It was a modern, stylish upper floor unit with a balcony that looked across Second Avenue to the inner harbour. The golf course with holes stretching along the water in Scottish links fashion dominated the opposite shore.

The apartment was nicer than his Vancouver digs, but he'd made no progress turning it into a home. He couldn't honestly claim he'd not had time to go furniture shopping, so his inertia might indicate a lack of commitment. He chose the office over sitting at home facing that possibility.

Simon was now working on the assumption the unidentified baby girl died within a month or two of her birth in the period between 1950 and 1965. Her expertly embalmed body, wrapped in a long piece of linen, had been entombed in the cabinet by removing two panels. The minor damage was effectively hidden by the sink unit. The insertion could have been accomplished before the sink unit was installed in 1962 or at a later date by temporarily dismantling part of the sink's cabinet. Mr. Ellis had shown this could be accomplished without further damage to either unit. But the perpetrator required access to a locked room for at least an hour when moderate noise would go unnoticed. That suggested someone with knowledge of the church and the comings and goings of the clergy and other staff.

Simon needed the results of DNA and other laboratory analyses before sinking his teeth into his refocused investigation. He turned to the probably unrelated mystery of Josh Corkum, Nicole Adams, and Edward Beardsley. He had no trouble finding the New England college where Nicole and Edward were undergraduates. Additional digging yielded the police department report of an incident resulting in the arrest of a group of twenty first-year students. The incident, property damage from an unauthorized student party was initially treated as a serious crime because the students were required to post bail. One Joshua Corcoran, a second-year student at the college, posted bail for Nicole and two other female students. For reasons not explained in the brief report, all charges were dropped a few months later.

Canadian immigration records showed Joshua Corcoran, a U.S. citizen, currently resided in Hunter's Creek using the name Josh Corkum. A check with the local RCMP detachment confirmed they knew Corkum and Corcoran were the same person.

Questions about the identity of someone he'd approached as an expert wouldn't look good if the case came to trial. Further digging into Josh's history, however, indicated nothing sinister. Neither Josh Corkum nor Joshua Corcoran had a criminal record in either the United States or Canada.

Simon put that problem aside, and over the next few days focused on the identity of the baby and her parents. He collated information on the church congregation, the clergy and lay people who assisted in services, and workmen hired to work in and around the church. Meticulous records kept by the church eased the task, and he received good cooperation from Reverend Leslie and John Harvey. By week's end, he had a long list of names of people involved with the church.

Saturday, Simon spent another day with Nicole. They left Barrettsport in the late morning for a tour of Lunenburg, a small town along the coast towards Halifax. The only route took them inland to the town of Bridgewater and back to the coast along the LaHave River.

Lunenburg was the type of tourist-oriented coastal community Simon imagined Barrettsport would be when he first considered the place. Somewhat smaller than Barrettsport, it had a commercial harbour with several functioning marine yards and a fish processing plant. It also had a major tourist attraction, the Fisheries Museum of the Atlantic, and a public boardwalk along the waterfront. A number of large fishing boats called Lunenburg home, and the main street had numerous restaurants and other small businesses catering to the more casual tourists. Bluenose, the famous two-masted schooner featured on the Canadian dime was built in Lunenburg, and the replica, Bluenose II, was Lunenburg based.

He saw several bed and breakfasts offering overnight accommodation, but none of the formal resorts and five-star restaurants dominating the tourist industry in Barrettsport. The only building that looked like it belonged in Barrettsport was the red, black and white Lunenburg Academy, the iconic old school dominating a hillside on the way into town. It could easily pass for one of Barrettsport's resort hotels.

He and Nicole had lunch in one of the many harbour-front restaurants, visited the museum and strolled along the waterfront before watching harbour activity from a bench. It was a different sort of date because of Josh's proposal to Nicole the previous weekend. Nicole wouldn't initially tell Simon her reaction to the proposal, but her flirty demeanour had changed. Simon had been transformed from a potential lover into a newly arrived friend or visiting relative who needed an introduction to the neighbourhood. The change suited Simon, and he decided the Lunenburg waterfront was the ideal place to ask her about Josh Corkum and her college years.

"I don't care how much you ask, I'm not talking about that stupid party or the awful time I spent in jail," she replied after his initial inquiry.

"But I've learned it wasn't your parents, but one Joshua Corcoran who bailed you out. Also, Josh Corkum is actually Joshua Corcoran. Can't you help me understand their meaning?"

"Is this a police interrogation? It's unfair to grill me like this."

"If you want me to change the subject, I will. But, don't you want to help me understand?"

She slid down the bench, folded her arms across her chest, and stared at the boats moving about the harbour. "Why should I?"

"Because I've called on Josh as an expert, and I don't want questions about him. And more important, it would give you the opportunity to clarify your earlier statement."

She paused while a small sloop approached the dock, jibed and headed into the harbour. "I should have described those two horrible nights more carefully. I wasn't trying to lie, but I used the word bail in a less precise way than you do. My parents helped extract me from the whole situation. They paid for the lawyer who defended me, and costs for my share of the damage we caused. Josh's money got me out of jail, but it wasn't at risk. I wasn't planning to run away, and when the charges were dropped, he got his money back."

"That answers several questions. You're okay, aren't you?" Simon asked, sliding over and trying to comfort her, but she turned away.

"It's just an experience I'd rather forget."

He sighed as he considered the best way to change the subject. He settled on a topic he'd pondered for days, the lack of nightlife more sophisticated than the Causeway Pub. Fortunately, it was unrelated to his case.

She dismissed the lack of nightclubs, stressing that Halifax was only two hours away, and waxed poetic about private parties. "And the great outdoors, beautiful beaches and fishing towns like this to explore. If you're into organized activities, there are golf courses and the yacht club."

"Sort of domesticated existence?"

"We like our peaceful place where families and kids are important. It's not like we don't have parties or activities of the sort you're referring to, but they're mostly private parties and out of public view. The bigger towns have pubs with darts tournaments and karaoke competitions. And they bring in local bands most weekends. But it's quiet for someone from a big city."

"Not that different from everywhere else, really," Simon suggested, continuing his attempt to make amends for his ham-fisted pursuit of his police investigation at an inappropriate time. "But it's difficult to break into the world you've described."

She didn't respond, and they sat watching the harbour traffic for several minutes.

"I should explain about Josh," Nicole said while gazing at the water.

"It's up to you."

"Josh was starting second year when I arrived. He's really smart but wasn't taking courses leading to his degree; he just took courses that interested him. He was nice to me and my two friends, not hitting on us, just friendly and helpful. The morning of the party he told us we should give it a miss." She pointed at two boats that looked like they might collide, but one tacked away. "But we were young and foolish and looking for fun, so we went anyway. We thought we were in a public park, but we were on someone's property, and apparently, they'd trespassed in other years. The owner hadn't previously called the cops."

"But this time he did."

"That's what happened, and we ended up in jail after some guys got aggressive and started a fight."

Simon reached over and put his arm around her shoulders. She relaxed and leaned her head against him. "So, you were arrested for assaulting the police and resisting arrest."

"Yeah, trespassing, drunkenness, public nudity because one girl removed her top, assaulting an officer and resisting arrest. Totally unfair because all most of us did was trespass on this guy's property. And we didn't know we'd done that."

Simon tried for several minutes to find the right sympathetic words. It was difficult because he couldn't avoid implied criticism of the police and justice system in a foreign jurisdiction. And he had only the sketchiest understanding of the relevant facts. But his words appeared to help because Nicole sat up straighter and returned to a more pleasant subject.

"But we're supposed to be talking about Josh."

Simon nodded. "That won't be so depressing."

"As I said, Josh was there a year before me and still working on his B.A. when I graduated. A year later he moved to Canada and started working for a boat builder near here. After that, he set up his shop in Hunter's Creek. I didn't know he was in Canada until I saw him in town one day."

"So, he hasn't been in the boat building business very long?"

She turned toward Simon, slowly shaking her head. "He worked with a boat builder in his hometown in Maine since early in high school, then every summer during college and full time for the last four years. Boat

58

building has been his life since he was sixteen, that's almost half his lifetime."

"But he wasn't your boyfriend at college?"

"Now you're getting personal. Two of my girlfriends and I considered him to be our friend, someone to go to if we needed help or advice."

"Did you think he was gay?"

"We never thought that. He's not gay!"

Simon stopped to think. Their emotions were disturbing his generally logical thought processes. He sensed Josh wasn't gay, but somehow the conversation kept drifting into quagmires. "Okay, we should drop this. Is it time we left?"

She held out her hand to prevent him from standing. "One more thing we should clarify. Joshua Corcoran's family is wealthy, but he just wants to build boats. When he came here, his family insisted he didn't use the family name for his boat building operation. He got carried away and changed his name in annoyance. There's nothing sinister about it, just a family tiff."

"I really am sorry about how this conversation's gone, and I don't want us to have a tiff. Should we find somewhere for coffee, or simply be on our way?"

"We should go, but don't worry, I'm not upset. In fact, I'm relieved to have it out in the open."

Simon stood, offering his hand to help her up. "Back to your place or somewhere else?"

"You mean like Josh's boat works? Simon, you really aren't good at being subtle!"

"So, I should drop you there?"

"Yes, please. Josh and I are going out to dinner, and I said we'd be back by five."

"We better hit the road," Simon said after glancing at his watch. It was almost four. "Does this mean you're treating his proposal more seriously than you did at the garden party?"

She smiled as she tugged on his hand and skipped toward the car. "I'm not telling, at least not yet. But whatever happens, I must thank you."

Another confusing twist in the conversation, Simon thought as he increased his stride to keep up with her canter. "Why?"

"Because I knew I should wipe my hands of Teddy Beardsley, but I waffled, unwilling to act. Then you came along and, well, you made it easy to put Teddy behind me."

Simon snorted. "Happy I could be of service."

"Please, don't be nasty. It's not like you're thinking. I had no idea Josh would propose. It was a complete surprise, and until that moment I thought you and I could have fun together."

"It's okay, really it is. My perspective wasn't so different," Simon said, secretly relieved because his own behaviour had been no more honourable. They'd been using each other to help sort out personal issues, and these unexpressed factors had complicated everything.

"Does that mean we're still friends?"

"If you'll be honest with me. You're going to say yes to Josh, aren't you?"

She reached for his hand as they approached the car. "Don't say anything. It's still a secret."

Chapter Twelve

Banter from the constables and Mrs. Margaret Summerville, the civilian employee who actually ran the station, greeted Simon when he arrived Monday morning. Margaret started it by asking him about Nicole Adams, joking when he seemed puzzled she was even aware of their relationship. "In a town like Barrettsport, you can't date the same woman three weeks in a row without everyone knowing about it."

She even asked him when the wedding date would be before Simon's furrowed brow told her she'd gone too far with her teasing. "I'm only joking, but you must realize you can keep few secrets when it comes to relationships in our little town. And before you become defensive with me, you should know everyone says you're doing Nicole a huge favour. You're just what she needs, someone to drag her away from her fixation with that fool she moped over through four years of college."

"Edward Beardsley," Simon responded. "Was he such a bad person?"

"He left her in the lurch. That makes him bad in my book."

Simon retreated to his office, worried Margaret was less knowledgeable than she thought. She had a distorted view of Nicole's relationship with Teddy Beardsley, and the real romance between Nicole and Josh had apparently escaped her attention, at least for the moment.

He wondered how the townsfolk would judge his behaviour. Would they understand he was comfortable with the part he'd played in the soon to be announced romance? Or would they conclude he'd been slighted after getting Nicole over her fixation with Edward Beardsley? Margaret was making a lot of his role, and he didn't want Margaret or any others trying to hook him up with someone else.

The little episode reminded him of the main conundrum in his mystery. Margaret had demonstrated that nosy neighbours were everywhere in Barrettsport. How could a baby be born, live for several weeks, die and be interred in the sacristy without anyone knowing? Someone had to know. Why hadn't they come forward?

Simon had only been at his desk for a few minutes when someone who might show up on Margaret's romantic radar screen appeared in his doorway.

"Detective Goodyear, could you perhaps spare me a few minutes?"

Simon welcomed her to his office and pointing at the chair by his desk with a sweep of his hand. "Certainly, Constable Jackson."

Her distinctive accent reminded Simon she'd not lived in Nova Scotia for too many years. Her intonation was that of a working-class black African from England, but her vocabulary was anything but working class.

Chief DeWolfe had introduced Simon to all seven constables on the Barrettsport police force when he arrived. Diana Jackson was the only woman and the only one from what officialdom called a visible minority.

She took the proffered chair. "Thank you. I've been considering your case, Detective Goodyear, and I've unearthed something that might have escaped your attention."

"Please, there's no need for formality. Call me Simon."

"How about guv. That's what we called our superiors when we were being informal." She smiled, a flash of sparkling white teeth lighting up her ebony-coloured face.

"Guv is it? And what did your guv call you?"

"Stupid shite as often as not, or, if I was lucky, hey you!"

Simon laughed. "Neither of those is appropriate. So, Diana, what's your brilliant idea?"

"Mrs. Murphy's Convalescent Resort. I don't know if you're even aware of it. It's the medical facility on Shore Road catering to women with drug and alcohol addiction problems."

Simon smiled at her description. It more closely resembled one of the resort hotels than a hospital. "Yes, I've seen the place."

"In the 1950s it was a maternity home, where unwed mothers bore babies that were mostly given up for adoption."

She now had Simon's attention. "That's definitely an interesting lead, something that could be important. Thank you, I'll see the chief recognizes the initiative you've shown."

"I'd be grateful, but I'd really appreciate the opportunity to contribute by pursuing this on your behalf."

"And that won't interfere with your regular duties?"

"If you don't require an immediate answer, I'll endeavour to carve out the time."

"I'll give you a week, and we'll see if you've succeeded?"

She stood with the big smile on her face. "Thank you, Sir Simon, sir, I really appreciate this opportunity." She hurried out, worried, perhaps, Simon would change his mind, or Chief DeWolfe would arrive and veto the plan. At least she hadn't called him guv.

He watched the physically impressive officer as she strode away. She clearly spent time in the gym but was not one of those hard-bodied women he'd known in the past, ones who shed their femininity when they worked on their Ms. Universe physiques. Constable Jackson was strong and muscular but still feminine, perhaps because she was the mother of two young boys. Whatever the reason, she had an alluring mixture of muscles and curves. Simon wondered briefly if she had a significant other, but quickly banished the closely related thought. It was none of his business, and a relationship with Diana would be no better than one with Nicole.

First Nicole Adams and now Diana Jackson was rekindling his interest in romance, but he must cast his nets in other waters. He could chase the perky young school teacher he'd seen at the Witherspoon's garden party or a young woman who worked in one of the town's shops. And none of that love 'em and leave 'em macho stuff. He was thirty-two years old. He needed to settle down and plan for the long term.

The medical examiner's report with the results of DNA analysis brought Simon back to reality. It contained various details that might prove useful and one stunning observation. The DNA analysis suggested the baby's parents were very closely related—either siblings or first cousins who shared many DNA characteristics.

This surprising new piece of evidence arrived just before Chief DeWolfe demanded a progress report.

"If I can summarize," the chief stated after listening without comment to the details of Simon's investigation. "The deceased was a Caucasian girl, weeks old when she died. Her body was carefully preserved and placed in what at first appeared to be an inaccessible space. Your investigation showed how our perpetrator gained access. It shows he or she had significant knowledge of Anglican ritual and the

63

process of embalming, adequate carpentry skills, and good knowledge of the church, including spaces the congregation rarely sees."

"I didn't mention the bit about Anglican ritual. Otherwise, it sums up what we know about him."

"Vivian Leslie told me he had to understand their ritual. He followed their arcane procedures for wrapping a body." He paused, glancing at his copy of the medical examiner's report. "And it's mentioned in the report."

"I'll add it to my list of personal characteristics we're looking for. He or she also needed unimpeded access to normally inaccessible parts of the church when it was empty."

"The other significant observation," added the chief, continuing his summary, "is DNA evidence suggesting parents in an incestuous relationship."

"I only received that information this morning, and I haven't had an opportunity to assess it. It might indicate the responsible party was incensed by the idea of a baby from an incestuous relationship?"

Chief DeWolfe leaned back with his hands on the edge of his desk. "We shouldn't speculate, at least not yet. What's your plan?"

Simon paused before answering. He'd spent three entire weeks on a case that was unlikely to go anywhere. But the chief seemed determined to continue an investigation that could stir up a lot of animosity.

"Assuming it's worth pursuing. It may be an accidental death, and I suspect the prosecutor's office will not consider pursuing a murder charge."

"My overall opinion has not changed. We must identify the baby, and then decide how to proceed."

"I can't separate an investigation of the baby's identity from a search for the parents. And the facts suggest it was probably someone associated with Barrettsport's Anglican Church. Will that generate problems?"

"It shouldn't. We must investigate without concern for anyone's sensibilities. And I agree, you can't avoid investigating these people, but identifying the baby should be your focus."

*****

Police Constable Diana Jackson skipped down the front steps of the station and turned toward Mrs. Murphy's Convalescent Resort. She strode confidently along Second Avenue but didn't hurry. Travis, her

64

long-standing companion and surrogate father to her two boys, was on the job. He would look after them and ensure supper was ready when she arrived home.

Seven years earlier, she'd left a good criminal investigation job in Brighton to venture abroad with her husband and young son. They left Britain for Canada, and a new start away from the paternalism and thinly disguised racism they'd encountered in the old country.

Dreams and reality often fail to align, and he'd departed less than a year later leaving Diana pregnant and alone with a toddler to raise. After the birth of her second son, she took stock of her situation. Her parents had emigrated from Nigeria to the United Kingdom before she was born and raised her to adulthood in their new home. It was Diana's turn to make a fresh start, raising her two sons in her new Canadian home.

She was a trained policewoman with several years experience in criminal investigation. Finding a new job as a policewoman in Canada became her immediate goal. She'd soon won a competition for a constable position in Barrettsport. She'd enjoyed her five years in Barrettsport and had no interest in moving on. But being a regular constable was not her long-term ambition. She coveted a return to criminal investigation, and this case might be her big opportunity.

Carmen Fernandez, the manager of the convalescent hospital, met Diana in the lobby.

"I've been expecting a visit from the police," Ms. Fernandez said as she led the way to her office. "The care of young women awaiting the birth of unwanted babies is no longer an important function of this facility, but in the 1950s and 1960s, it was all we did."

As she followed Ms. Fernandez along the hallway, Diana wondered if she was about to receive a fabrication, a carefully edited cover-up, or something close to the real story. It didn't matter. Whatever she learned at Mrs. Murphy's Convalescent Resort would jumpstart her own investigation into the history of babies born during the period that interested Simon.

65

Chapter Thirteen

Simon's working hypothesis described a crime committed by someone from the local community who was familiar with, and had access to, St. George's Church. A brother, father or a double first cousin with four common grandparents impregnated someone. She carried the baby to term and give birth without public knowledge or registration. Then, after the baby died, someone deposited the body in the church.

The perpetrator required unfettered private access to the sacristy. He or she needed knowledge of the under-counter space and how to access it, as well as Anglican ritual and the procedures for embalming a corpse.

Simon began his search at the top of the hierarchy with the minister in charge between 1950 and 1965. According to John Harvey's history, the Reverend Gerald McKnight was a high church Anglican who favoured practices that were almost Roman Catholic. Mr. Harvey's history described these practices and compared them in the following chapter to the less formal ones during the tenure of Reverend Robert Fulton from 1980 until 2005. The distinctions John described made little sense to Simon. He could associate the use of incense by the Anglo-Catholics with Roman Catholic practices. Otherwise, the ritual during both periods seemed structured and formal compared to his limited understanding of Protestant churches.

McKnight was married at the beginning of his tenure, but his wife died in 1958. They had no children, and after retiring from active ministry, he lived as a monk in an Anglican monastery in Quebec. Simon imagined a scenario where Reverend McKnight is disconsolate about the death of his wife, seeks solace with some woman, producing a child who dies in infancy. He hides the body and disappears into a monastery to atone for his sins. But the DNA evidence says this cannot be. His biography in John Harvey's book says he was an only child of a couple living in Ontario. Unless John made important errors in his research, Reverend McKnight was in the clear.

The history described Reverend McKnight as a scholar who wrote several theological monographs. Mr. Harvey described him as an austere authoritarian figure who oversaw the church ritual and presented sermons each Sunday but left parish duties to a succession of assistants. They worked at the Barrettsport church for two to four years before moving to their own parishes.

Simon next considered the seven assistant ministers. They were all male in this era of male clergy, and if there had been women ministers, an Anglo-Catholic congregation wouldn't have welcomed them. Some of these assistant ministers were married; others were single during their sojourns in Barrettsport but married later.

He spent three days resolving the history of Reverend McKnight and his seven assistants but came up empty. He unearthed no sign of incestuous relationships that could have produced a baby girl. All seven assistant ministers were alive and living in Canada. He could procure DNA samples if he generated the appropriate arguments.

The parish council members and the sacristans and various lay people who performed similar functions were next on Simon's list. These mostly older men had families and well-established reputations. Not likely one of them fathered a baby with a sister, daughter, or double first cousin without it becoming known, but he couldn't dismiss them entirely. He transferred them to a list of secondary possibilities and put it aside for the moment.

Finally, he had Nicole prepare computerized lists of the congregation members during the period. That gave him a long list of candidates and no clear way to focus on likely suspects.

Diana Jackson resolved one uncertainty when she produced a detailed report of her investigation of Mrs. Murphy's Convalescent Resort. She included the report of a formal investigation of activities at the maternity home written in 1953 after the fiasco related to the Ideal Maternity Home in East Chester.

"Everything until 1953 was investigated with no problems uncovered," Simon suggested after perusing Diana's summary of the government investigations.

67

"And I interviewed the current manager. She prepared records for the rest of your time period. It checks out."

"But if there was a problem, they wouldn't have recorded it."

"Orchestrating a cover-up would have been difficult because government regulations were tightened after the East Chester fiasco. I looked at their documentation, newspaper accounts, and other records I could access and found no indication of impropriety at the home. It's in my report."

Simon looked at the size of Diana's report. "I'll read it, of course, but you're telling me there's nothing for me."

"I think not," Diana concluded as she prepared to leave. She sounded disappointed and Simon realized she'd hoped to find something that would justify her continued involvement in the investigation. A campaign to land a new job as a detective constable drove much of her effort. She was keen and competent, and Simon liked the idea of an assistant. He silently vowed to help her achieve her ambition.

Diana's comments about newspaper reports got Simon thinking about his own library research, and the discussions he'd had with Nicole Adams, Caroline Garrett, and others. He'd pieced together a lot of innuendo about affairs involving members of the town's governing families. If he believed the rumours, Barrettsport could give a run to any TV soap opera. But the gossip wasn't helping Simon solve his problem. The affairs led away from rather than towards incestuous relationships because the reports generally alluded to relationships outside the inner circle of families.

The maternity home discussion reminded Simon of another aspect of his research. A surprising number of young relatives visited the Barrettsport families for extended periods every summer during and after the Second World War. The town's weekly newspaper contained pictures of groups of kids with one or more identified as so-and-so's cousin, nephew or niece.

One photo showed a tall skinny ten or twelve-year-old Alexander Merrick standing beside a chubby girl a year or two younger. She was identified as Linda Turnbull, a member of the Adams clan. They were smiling as if sharing a joke, which probably made the photo stick in Simon's mind. Comments he'd heard around town suggested Alexander was a difficult child who was withdrawn and gloomy. Perhaps the photographer caught Alexander in a rare moment of happiness.

68

The image of Mayor Richard Merrick pumping him for information at Tim Hortons some days earlier popped into Simon's head. Was the mayor worried about something in his brother's past?

Through this period after Josh's proposal, Nicole seemed to think she had a duty to give Simon a crash course on life on Nova Scotia's south shore. Josh and his assistant were busy getting a yacht completed by some deadline, leaving Nicole free to act as Simon's tour guide. On one of these Saturday outings, she continued, as was her wont, to talk about the Barrettsport families.

"It isn't easy growing up with the expectations," she explained on their way home from an afternoon spent around Shelburne, a town an hour's drive southwest of Barrettsport.

"All parents have expectations for their kids," Simon suggested.

"Everyone isn't expected to contribute to the success of their hometown and look after the less fortunate citizens."

"Doesn't your church teach everyone to do that?"

"But others aren't expected to marry someone in a narrow range of suitable matches and make such large commitments to their town."

He turned down a small road toward Summerville Beach Provincial Park. This didn't sound like a conversation for busier traffic he expected on the final stage of their journey. They also had time to kill before the dinner reservation he'd made. "It can't be that bad. You do live the lord of the manor lifestyle."

"I don't want you to think I'm ungrateful, but the families' expectations for their offspring are too much," she began as they strolled onto the beach. "They expect us to continue to live in the throwback society they've built and take on responsibility for everyone in town. And most annoying, they expect us either to marry within the families or into a certain culture of New England families they identify with. I mean why shouldn't I marry a nice bloke like you if I want to?"

Simon couldn't resist the opportunity to tease. "What! Are you proposing? I thought you already had Edward Beardsley and Josh Corkum fighting over you. Isn't that enough?"

Nicole stopped and clamped her hands on her hips. "Oh, Simon, you are a dear, but I'm not making a proposal. I'm explaining I couldn't even if I wanted to."

"Okay, why don't you carry on with your explanation?"

He was intrigued by her change in attitude. She'd always defended the family traditions, and a few days earlier during their ill-fated

69

conversation on the Lunenburg boardwalk, suggested she felt free to choose any husband she wanted. These subtle changes might prove useful in helping him understand the community's dynamics.

"Take my family for example. I have two older brothers, each married into the 'acceptable' New England families. One lives with his wife and children in Barrettsport. He's a doctor and the other, also with two children, is a financier in Halifax. They visit every few weeks and he's involved in several Barrettsport activities."

"I see, what about the mayor's family? He's one of the family members I met before your Victoria Day bash, so a good place to go next."

"They follow the approved model. His older brother refused to follow the proper behaviour and was banished. The mayor married one of the Smith girls. They obviously stayed here and now he's mayor."

Nicole deviated onto a well-marked path into the piping plover's breeding habitat. She paused at a viewing station. "They have three kids, two boys and a girl, in university or recently graduated. None are married yet, but one boy is engaged to a cousin of the Wexlers, and the others are reportedly going the New England spouse route."

"I heard the mayor had a third brother," Simon said, encouraging her to continue. The conversation was becoming more relevant to his investigation. He didn't want her to stop.

Nicole shook her head. "A sister with Down's syndrome. They sent her to a home for the handicapped when she was a child. I suspect she died because she's never mentioned. If she's still alive she'd be almost sixty."

"Down's syndrome is so sad. I don't know how parents cope."

"True, but many other afflictions are as hard on families. Take, for example, the Wexler brothers. They each had a child who died from childhood cancers. They fit the pattern I've been describing; the brothers are both prominent figures married to daughters of other Barrettsport families. Their little sister was a rebel, interested in folk music and jazz. She had a scandalous affair with a folk singer but is now an upright member of society. Youthful indiscretions are forgiven if you put them behind you and accept your responsibility to the community. That's how it works."

She described the marital arrangements of other family members after they returned to the highway. When they arrived at the new seafood restaurant by the Barrettsport town pier, Simon had inside information on a number of new candidates for parents of his mystery

70

baby. Later, he thought as he raised his wine glass, I'll correlate these latest findings with my list of sacristans, vergers and other identifiable church dignitaries from the 1950s and '60s.

Chapter Fourteen

That evening, at home with his thoughts, Simon recalled their discussion. He added Nicole's observations to the notes and lists he'd made after sifting through the records he'd found and produced a new master list of potential parents. Any fathers with daughters or brothers with sisters were possibilities, so he demanded some additional indication before he added an individual to this list of prime candidates. As more information became available, he expected the list to grow.

The first name he added was Alexander Merrick. He was born in 1937 more than ten years before his brother Richard, Barrettsport's current mayor, in 1948, and Felicity, their little sister with Down's syndrome, in 1950. Simon's research marked Alexander as an exceptionally bright child with a phenomenal memory and interests in various scientific subjects far advanced for his years but no social skills. Some people referred to him as an idiot savant, and perhaps he had a form of autism, but Simon found no official medical diagnosis. He did, however, learn Alexander graduated from a private high school then disappeared for several years before returning to Barrettsport with an interest in theology early in the 1960s. Apparently, he became as obsessed with theology as he had been with various scientific fields when younger. His friendship with Reverend McKnight, the Anglo-Catholic rector at St. George's Church was mentioned in John Harvey's church history. A few years later he disappeared again, and Simon found no more recent information. An aunt; his father's much younger sister, made Alexander a potential candidate. She was a few years older than Alexander and disappeared from public view during the period when Alexander returned to Barrettsport. The families were so inbred that

Simon couldn't disregard the possibility a baby produced by Alexander and his aunt had the genetic characteristics they required.

His second potential suspect was one of several members of an eccentric family living on a farm between Barrettsport and Liverpool. The marginal farm had an extensive vegetable garden, some pasture land, and a much larger woodlot. It provided a meagre living for the patriarch of the family, Jack Rice, his wife, her spinster sister, and his nine children. He was a religious, but private, man who brought his whole family to church at St. George's Anglican Church every Sunday in the 1960s. The family lived well removed from any neighbours and kept to themselves. None of the girls finished school and efforts by school truancy and welfare officials to visit the family were always rebuffed. Simon couldn't exclude the possibility Jack Rice or one of his three sons had established an incestuous relationship with one of his six daughters that produced an undocumented baby. They remained on his list.

His third possibility was a Barrettsport man, a Mr. Gerald Clarke, whose parents died in a 1958 car accident when he was nineteen, leaving him responsible for two younger sisters. The older sister married and left home not long after the accident. The man and his younger sister lived together in Bridgewater until they disappeared from the public record between 1965 and 1970.

Another possibility was Georgina Killing, a teenage girl from Upper Barrettsport who disappeared in 1958 for months before resurfacing. No one explained her absence and Simon couldn't discount the possibility she'd borne a child fathered by either her older brother or her father.

Several other teenage girls became pregnant during this period, but none of their stories were as mysterious. Next, he recalled the saga of Mildred Wexler, student radical and coffee house proprietor. Simon added them to his list of investigative possibilities.

Finally, there was Jim Ellis, the man who discovered the body. He realized what he'd discovered before anyone else did, he had the carpentry skills needed to hide the body, and he was the right age. Jim wouldn't have been a member of the St. George's Church congregation, but he grew up one hundred kilometres away in East Chester. He and his wife Barbara married in 1965 when he was only twenty-two and her maiden name was Ellis. They might have been cousins.

Simon drove to the Rice farm on Monday, June twenty-fifth, a beautiful summer day with no sign of the almost ubiquitous fog. Simon observed

73

an old man, presumably Jack Rice, the family patriarch, sitting in a rocking chair on the front porch of the family homestead. Mr. Rice made no effort to rise when Simon parked his car and approached the porch. The old weather-beaten house needed painting, but it looked straight and square and structurally sound. The rugged-looking furniture on the porch was not derelict, and the wind chimes and dream catchers hanging from the roof beams gave it a homey appearance.

"Hello, Mr. Rice," Simon called out from the bottom of the stairs.

"Yeah, what's it to you?" he barked before Simon completed his thought.

"My name is Simon Goodyear, and I'm with the Barrettsport Police Department. Could we have a word?"

"Martha," the man bellowed turning toward the front door. He may have been old and frail-looking, but his voice was strong. "You'd best fetch John."

Seconds later, a plain-looking middle-aged woman pushed the door open while drying her hands on her apron.

"This here fellow says he's with the police, and he wants to talk to John."

"Are you from the Mounties?" Martha asked while giving Simon the once-over.

"No, ma'am, the Barrettsport Police Department, and I'd like a word with Mr. Jack Rice about something that happened at the Anglican Church many years ago."

"I see," she replied. "It will be best if I fetch John. You hold tight, and I'll be right back."

Simon stood at the bottom of the steps until another man, somewhat younger than Jack, approached from a nearby barn.

"You best come up, and we can sort this out," he suggested as he climbed to the porch deck and pulled two chairs closer to the rocker.

"I'm John Rice and this is my father Jack. You've met my wife, Martha, and the only other person here today is my sister Becky. What is it you want? If it's our kids you're after, you're out of luck. They're in Liverpool delivering early produce to the market and doing some shopping."

"As I already tried to explain, I'm looking for information about the Barrettsport Anglican church from the 1950s and 1960s. I understand your family attended services there."

"Spiteful place," sputtered Jack. "Should have stopped going there sooner, but my old grandmother wanted us to be Anglicans."

Simon was puzzled by the interjection but tried to ignore it as he continued his explanation. "We found the body of a baby girl who died in the 1950s or 1960s. I'm asking everyone I can find who attended church during that period if they know anything that might help me identify the baby."

"I was only a kid when we stopped going there," John replied. "Dad, what about you? Remember anything useful?"

"Papists!" Jack exclaimed. "The minister might as well have been one of them Roman Catholics. They treated us like lepers. No one in that damn town would say a word to us."

John shrugged his shoulders and turned to Simon. "We won't be much help. Weren't welcome, but Dad respected his grandparents' wishes. They were Anglicans and wanted their children and grandchildren to follow the faith. Dad tried to do what his grandma wanted. Isn't that right?"

"She was a good woman. Martha!" Jack bellowed. "Fetch the photo album."

"Would she have attended the church in Barrettsport?" Simon asked Jack, but he ignored the question, staring into the distance.

John answered for him as Martha emerged from inside the house with a large, red, leather-bound photo album. "Small chapel on the reserve and a roving minister who conducted services."

Simon admired an old photo of an indigenous woman standing before a plain wooden building with a prominent cross. He glanced at the dream catchers on the Rice's porch, took a deep breath and broached a sensitive topic. "We're also searching for the parents."

"I knew it," Jack burst out. "You're trying to pin this on us. Get off my property. Now!"

"But sir," Simon retorted. "I'm not trying to pin anything on anyone. If I was, what you and John told me proves you aren't the father."

"How's that?" John asked.

"The parents of that child didn't have indigenous blood. If you have aboriginal ancestors, none of you can be the parent. A simple test would prove it."

"We're Mi'kmaq and proud of it, but I'm not doing no tests." That was Jack Rice's final word. He made a show of clamping his mouth shut before turning away.

Simon departed a few minutes later with addresses for several of John's siblings and an agreement he would visit the hospital in Liverpool for a DNA test.

75

Chapter Fifteen

Sunday, July first was Canada's national holiday and the day of the second formal Barrettsport summer garden party. At the gathering, Mayor Richard Merrick aided Simon's quest by asking him what he thought of the prominent families. Simon couldn't afford to pass up the opportunity, so he launched into questions about Mayor Merrick's family.

"Our family isn't typical," the mayor said. He sipped his scotch as he pondered his reply to Simon's question. "My parents married before World War II and had my brother before Dad enlisted in the army. My sister and I were born much later after the war ended. Dad had only one sister so we've been less prolific than most families."

"What about your mother, was she also a Barrettsport family member?"

The mayor laughed. "She's an Adams like your new girlfriend."

"Nicole's not my girlfriend. She's been generous with her time, helping me learn about Barrettsport and the general geography and history of this part of Nova Scotia. She's made it clear her affections lie elsewhere, but she's been a good friend, and I hope it stays that way."

"That's good because today we're expecting an announcement affecting Nicole, and I hoped it wouldn't surprise you."

Simon was confident he had the inside track on any news related to Josh and Nicole. "No sir, it won't be a shock. But what about your brother, he hasn't remained like Nicole tells me all good sons and daughters should?"

"True. The majority make significant contributions to Barrettsport society, but some like my brother don't belong. He's gifted in many ways but has absolutely zero social skills. He made the correct choice by establishing his life elsewhere after college."

"So, he's not someone destined to be mayor."

"Definitely not," the mayor replied, laughing. "Being mayor demands good social skills and a willingness to bend your ideas to suit the majority. My brother could manage neither of those."

"What happened to him?"

"He chose to be a religious scholar, living a hermit-like existence in various places writing theological treatises. He will help people in need, but he's intolerant of those who don't meet his strict definition of good."

"So hard to live with," Simon suggested.

Someone thumped the mayor on the back before posing a question about civic politics. The interruption gave Simon a chance to consider their conversation in Tim Hortons. Everything he learned about Alexander pointed to a possible sinister interpretation of that conversation.

The mayor turned to Simon as his intervener stumbled away. "Where were we?"

"Talking about your brother; I suggested he must have been hard to cope with."

"That's an understatement. I consider myself a basically good Christian who's generous with his time and money, but nothing I did met with Alexander's approval. The same for my parents and everyone else I know. None of us met Alexander's strict standards."

"From what I've heard, you're almost universally acknowledged as a superior mayor."

"I hope you're right because there's an election in the fall, and I'm up for re-election."

A woman who'd been hovering nearby stepped forward. "It's a foregone conclusion, isn't it? Mayors and selectmen are always from the families and always re-elected."

Mayor Merrick turned to the interloper. "Hello Cynthia, have you met our new detective? Cynthia, this is Detective Simon Goodyear. Simon, Cynthia Ettinger. Cynthia's a radical in our midst. She has the crazy notion she can dislodge one of the selectmen and get herself elected as our first selectwoman."

"Damn right. I'm going to shake up this town, bringing it kicking and screaming into the twenty-first century."

The conversation drifted into other topics, and Simon learned nothing more from the mayor. Someone else said Alexander Merrick left Barrettsport after an argument with his father about Felicity, his little sister.

Later, Josh and Nicole cornered Simon, and they had a drink together before another young woman approached Nicole and whispered something in her ear. Nicole looked at Simon then shrugged her shoulders. "I'm staying here and entertaining these two."

"Yeah, right," the other girl muttered, "if you really want to entertain them you would come with me." She gave Simon a coquettish look and disappeared toward the swimming pool where a large noisy crowd had gathered.

"What's happening?" Simon asked as the decibel level increased.

"One of our many traditions," Nicole replied. "The young women are entertaining the young men."

She stood without explaining the form of entertainment. "I'm going for another drink; can I bring you guys anything?"

"What in God's name was that about?" Simon asked Josh as noises associated with people diving or jumping into the pool punctuated the general hooting and hollering of the pool-side crowd.

"It must seem strange to an outsider," Josh said as Nicole walked toward the bar. "We, like everyone else, have our traditions, and some are unusual. They can be as wild and crazy as the ones you hear about students in university dorms or Hollywood stars. The biggest difference is we conduct our outlandish activities in private, not in public. It's a safe environment, no one's overstepping boundaries, and everyone lives his, or in this case her, fantasies. No one's hurt and no harm's done."

"But what's actually happening?"

"The young women are entertaining the young men by stripping off their party dresses and having a swim."

"And the other woman expected Nicole to participate with you by the pool egging her on."

"That's right and you too. In fact, you're welcome to check it out, but it's not my thing. I've always declined to play my part."

Simon shook his head as the hooting and hollering reached a crescendo. "Well good for you because the whole business seems sexist, coercing women who are barely older than girls to strip down in public."

"It's not like that. Young women started this, and none of the participants are unwilling. You saw how keen that woman was. It's their

79

idea, and no one is coercing them. Some of the stodgier men want to stop it, but they won't succeed because this little show has widespread support."

Nicole returned, placing three glasses of wine on the table. "I hope you now see that as well as all the perks and privileges, we also have responsibilities and obligations."

"Does that mean you've participated in this particular stunt in the past?"

"Oh, yes, pretty much every summer party since I was eighteen. It's something we look forward to, our opportunity to tease and torment young men who take their responsibilities too seriously. I thought about participating after Beverly appeared." She paused and looked at Simon. His brow furrowed as he tried to comprehend this latest revelation about Barrettsport society.

"I imagined leading you to the front of the crowd and performing for your benefit," Nicole said, smiling broadly. She apparently thought this activity was an innocent lark, but Simon couldn't get his head around her attitude.

"For me, you're kidding!"

"Definitely for you. Josh and I are in your debt for bringing us together, and it would be my way of showing you how much we appreciate what you've done for us."

"But I haven't done anything."

"You have. I don't know how you did it, but you've been the catalyst that's brought us together, and we're truly thankful."

Simon turned toward Josh. "And what would you have done if she'd led me to the pool to watch while she did a striptease for me and all the other men?"

Nicole broke in before Josh could answer. "Come, Josh, we have an announcement to make."

"Encouraged her," Josh said over his shoulder as he followed Nicole to a suitable vantage point to formally announce their engagement once everyone cavorting about the pool returned.

80

Chapter Sixteen

Simon entered the Barrettsport Police Station Monday morning somewhat hungover from the celebrations after Nicole and Josh gave him far too much credit for bringing them together. It was a good hangover, accompanying the realization his friendship with Nicole helped her decide. He also realized it was helping him overcome the messed up personal relationships that triggered his move to Nova Scotia. Soon, he should be able to abandon his self-imposed exile from romantic attachments. He didn't know how he would express his appreciation, but one thing was clear. He wouldn't be entertaining Nicole and her friends by swimming in his underwear at a garden party.

In his office with his third cup of morning coffee, he turned his attention to the search for the baby girl's parents. He'd spent days working through his suspects one at a time. He'd eliminated the Rice's first, and by July second, several other dominoes had fallen into place. Gerald Clarke provided him with a logical, well-documented story and a DNA sample that would settle the matter with certainty. Simon also eliminated Georgina Killing and the other girls with teenage pregnancies. The social service agencies that looked after placement of their unwanted babies provided good documentation for all of them.

Nicole had described Mildred Wexler's chequered past with unspecified indiscretions during and after her university years. A record check showed the fifty-eight-year-old spinster would have been fifteen at the end of the 1950 to 1965 window for the baby's death. Simon found no missing time from school or anything else to suggest a problem during her teenage years that could have produced an illegitimate baby. He found newspaper articles describing a relationship with a musician, and a coffee shop they operated in Barrettsport. But this interesting episode in Barrettsport's history occurred in 1973, so irrelevant for his investigation.

Jim Ellis was next on his list. Simon caught up with him Wednesday afternoon in the church where he was putting the finishing touches on the cupboard he'd created in the sacristy.

"Does it pass muster?" Jim asked, swinging his new doors shut as Simon entered the room.

"Beautiful, it looks like they've been there all along. Hard to believe you achieved such a good match."

"New brass hinges and latch, but the wood is original. I stained the newly cut surfaces. You don't see them unless the doors are open, so slight discrepancies in the colour don't matter."

"I'd say it's pretty damn professional. When you said you were only a rough carpenter the day we first met, I suspect you sold yourself short."

"This wasn't a difficult job." He stood facing Simon. "But you aren't here to admire my work, are you?"

"I have a few questions related to my search for the baby's identity."

"About the discovery, or about something else?"

"Something else. The parents were very closely related, and I've learned you and your wife were cousins, so I need your story."

Jim hesitated. His furrowed brow indicated his consternation as he considered the implications of Simon's request. "We didn't live here until the 1990s, and anyway, we couldn't have children."

"But we have very few genetic possibilities, and I'm checking all double first cousins."

"I don't even understand that term."

"Cousins so closely related they have all four grandparents in common."

Jim snorted as he packed tools in his ubiquitous satchel. "Then Barbara and I are double first cousins. You want a DNA sample to show I'm not the father?"

"That would be best, but I can't insist. I'd also like your story if you don't mind telling me."

"I'm not the baby's father. If I must provide you with a DNA sample to prove it, that's what I'll do."

"And your story?"

Jim hesitated, and Simon considered the possibility of Jim refusing to tell his story. He sighed with relief when Jim chose to continue.

82

"In 1961 after high school, I left my East Chester home looking for work in Ontario. At first, I lived in Toronto with an uncle and his family. Their daughter; Barbara, had polio. She was crippled and didn't get out much, but we fell in love and decided to marry. It wasn't a popular decision, but we persisted. We knew first cousins shouldn't have kids, but it didn't matter because there were issues related to her polio that made having a baby inappropriate. She had her tubes tied before we married. That was 1965 and we hadn't made love before our wedding night, so no babies from us. We lived in Ontario until I retired in 1996, and we moved here."

"How often did you visit Nova Scotia while you lived in Ontario?"

"Most years, sometimes twice in a year. We had relatives down east and family events to attend."

"Did those visits include Barrettsport?"

"Sometimes. I never visited this church, but Barbara attended a few services."

Simon arranged for collection of a DNA sample, and, after he returned to his office, made a few inquiries to verify Jim's story. It all checked out.

This process of elimination left him with Alexander Merrick or someone who hadn't yet surfaced during his scouring of the local history.

Merrick fit the picture forming in Simon's mind almost perfectly. He was an extremely bright loner obsessive about anything that interested him. If he developed an interest in embalming, he would have studied it to death and known how to preserve the body in a professional manner. He was familiar with Barrettsport's Anglican Church and spent many hours there in his youth. Finally, he had the opportunity for an illicit affair with his slightly older aunt who disappeared from Barrettsport in 1961. She returned a year later married to an outsider.

He needed a DNA sample to either clear or implicate Alexander Merrick. That meant he needed to locate Alexander and procure a sample. But his brother, Mayor Richard Merrick, claimed he had no idea where to locate him. In fact, Richard seemed unaware of anything related to his brother or his sister. Did that make sense for ruling families obsessed with their pseudo-hereditary dominance?

83

Chapter Seventeen

The next morning, Reverend Leslie added an entrant to Simon's search.

"May I come in?" she asked from his office doorway. "I learned something we thought you should know."

Simon waved her into his office. "We?"

"John Harvey and I." She settled into the chair Simon indicated and stared momentarily into space. Then, she shook her head and focused on Simon. "Yesterday, I visited Mr. Jerome Dobson, our oldest active parishioner. He's been unwell, and I dropped by to see how he was doing. I was hardly in the door when he began ranting about someone called Bartholomew Barrett."

Simon turned and punched the name into his computer. "What do we know about Bartholomew Barrett? Is he related to the original Barretts who settled Barrettsport?"

"No idea. But Jerome thinks it's serious. He insisted Mr. Barrett had not been brought to task."

"Right. You consider this relevant to my investigation?"

Reverend Leslie hesitated again, staring at a steeple formed by her fingertips, a pose Simon was beginning to associate with her. "Yes."

"Something Mr. Dobson said?"

"No, something John Harvey said."

"Ah, yes, John. How does he come into this?"

"I phoned him to learn if he knew about Bartholomew Barrett."

"And he apparently did."

"He said Mr. Barrett was a controversial figure from your time period. John chose to exclude him until he fills gaps in Barrett's story. Then he'll add him to his history."

Simon stood and strode to the whiteboard where he had columns of information for individuals he'd considered as potential parents. He squeezed the words Bart Barrett into space on the extreme right. "Why didn't John tell me about this controversial guy?"

"I suspect he simply forgot. Now, he wants to make amends and fill you in on Sexton Barrett."

"Sexton? I don't recall either you or John saying anything about anyone called sexton. And aren't sextons associated with grave digging?"

"In times past, the church sexton oversaw the church graveyard and burials. Nowadays, churches appoint a council member to manage the building and grounds. He, or possibly she, is often given the title sexton. In our church, one of the congregational members of Parish Council looks after these functions, but we don't give him a title."

"But you could call him sexton, just like you say Elizabeth Morrow is the sacristan. And in the 1950s and 1960s your church did have a sexton, and at one time, he was Bartholomew Barrett."

"That's what John tells me. You should ask him to explain."

"Or visit him at his home and have more chili for lunch."

Vivian Leslie smiled, masking the furtive look she'd had until then. "I suppose you could."

Half an hour later, Simon was sitting on John Harvey's living room sofa with a coffee cup in his hand. Chili was not on his agenda. Simon hoped to soon be back in his office investigating this latest twist in his puzzle before returning to his primary goal, convincing Chief DeWolfe they should pursue Alexander Merrick.

"I owe you an apology," John Harvey said from his recliner chair across the room. "I completely forgot about Mr. Barrett, an unforgivable lapse as he was an unusual character, and someone you should have known about. It also shows a serious flaw in my scholarship. I knew he was an important figure, but I had so many questions I deleted him from my manuscript. I have an extensive file, and I will reintroduce him once I answer them."

"These things happen, and you warned me your book was a work in progress."

"But that means it might have gaps and unanswered questions, not a complete purging of his name."

John's elaborate *mea culpa* puzzled Simon, and he wondered what it might mean. But he was anxious to address the immediate task of learning about Bartholomew Barrett. He could consider John's motives, and those of Reverend Leslie, at a later date.

"So, what can you tell me about Mr. Barrett?"

"Best thing I can do is send you my file. You can add it to the one I already sent you."

"Will you summarize it for me?"

"I reviewed the material after talking to Vivian. Bartholomew Barrett first appears in records I found for the spring of 1962. He joined the St. George's congregation immediately after arriving here. Within a year he'd been appointed to the Parish Council, the church's governing body, and officially named sexton at his third meeting."

Simon scrutinized John's expression. His odd demeanour suggested he was delivering a prepared speech without the banter characterizing their earlier conversation.

"Tell me about this sexton business," Simon said. "Mrs. Leslie told me he's the council member responsible for managing the building and grounds. Under the current regime, these duties are handled by one or more members, but no one is officially titled sexton."

"That's correct, and the way it's usually organized, but Reverend McKnight was a more formal minister in a more formal time. And that spring, two council members, including the sexton, resigned. Nominating new council members made sense, but Mr. Barrett was an odd choice."

"Why's that?"

"First, he'd only been a congregation member for a year. Council usually comprises long-standing members. Second, Bartholomew Barrett was a boisterous, colourful character. Not the type you'd expect in such a job, or acceptable to Reverend McKnight and his conservative congregation."

"No, I suppose not. What about the two resignations? Was there a split within the council?"

John laughed as he shook his head. He finally appeared to be abandoning his script. "No indication of that. Two aging men, and one was definitely ailing."

"But something about the story caused you to exclude him from your history."

"I needed more information. Where this guy came from? How he became a central figure so quickly? Why Reverend McKnight would

86

support him? I don't see how these questions affect your investigation, but I want to answer them before I write him into my book."

"You say he had Reverend McKnight's support."

"Hard to believe he had such a rapid ascension without it."

"Indeed, and the question of why Reverend McKnight would support such an inappropriate person could be interesting for my investigation."

Chapter Eighteen

In the water taxi back to Barrettsport, Simon sat outside basking in the summer sunshine. The taxi, a thirteen-metre-long launch with inside seating for a dozen people, was the total extent of Barrettsport's public transit system. It plied the harbour between Barrettsport and Hunter's Creek on an hourly basis from six a.m. until midnight.

In April, May, and June, his first three months on the east coast, there had been occasional warm sunny days, but many more cold, blustery ones. People said spring was not the best season along Nova Scotia's Atlantic coast, but he hadn't appreciated how drawn-out the almost wintry season would be.

Then, suddenly, it was summer. The weather had been perfect for the Canada Day garden party, and today he hadn't needed even a light jacket during the fifteen-minute crossing.

He thought about Reverend Leslie and John Harvey's odd demeanours as they described Bartholomew Barrett. They seemed anxious to help but apologetic. John failed to mention someone who might be important, but why had Vivian Leslie been equally contrite? She'd passed on information she learned within hours.

What bothered them? Barrett was an important name in Barrettsport. Might the mysterious Bartholomew Barrett be related to the Merricks or Ettingers, the descendants of Cornelius Barrett? Or were John and Reverend Leslie suppressing another link to the 'families'?

Perhaps the church hierarchy knew something unsavoury about the relationship between Bartholomew Barrett and Reverend McKnight. Could John have discovered something during his research and mentioned it to Vivian when she called him yesterday? Then if she withheld the information when she talked to Simon, it might explain her demeanour.

But could that problem, or another Bartholomew-related secret, bear on his case? A visit to Jerome Dobson, Vivian's source, might shed light on the situation.

Mr. Dobson lived in the little apartments, a three-storey building on Seventh Avenue near the top of the hill backstopping the town. The only other apartment building, the seven-storey edifice on Second Avenue where Simon lived, was called the big apartments.

Simon noticed the smattering of sailboats in the harbour when he paused in front of the building waiting for Dobson to welcome him. Must be nice, he thought, to have time for a leisurely sail on a weekday morning. He'd done some sailing when he lived in Vancouver. Maybe, once he settled down, he could consider a small sailboat of his own.

Jerome Dobson released the entranceway lock and Simon climbed the stairs to his third-floor apartment.

"Thank you for agreeing to talk to me on such short notice," Simon said to the dapper older gent waiting in the hallway. He was neither as old nor as frail as Simon expected from Vivian's description. He looked quite chipper and capable of climbing the three flights of stairs to his apartment.

Jerome smiled. "I feel honoured, two visitors in two days. Might help me shake this nagging cough. The weather has also improved, so I have no excuse. I should venture forth and discover if my cronies are still kicking."

Yes, definitely chipper, Simon thought as Jerome led the way into his apartment and pointed to a sitting room chair. "How can I help the Barrettsport Police Department?"

"As you may know, I've been investigating the death of a baby girl whose body was placed in St. George's Church in the 1950s or 1960s. During my investigation, I identified the main players in the church. But I apparently missed one important person, one you brought to Reverend Leslie's attention yesterday."

"I assumed it had to be about Bartholomew Barrett. I must apologize to Reverend Leslie. My outburst was uncalled for. I overreacted when her visit brought back an unpleasant memory."

More apologies, Simon thought as he encouraged Mr. Dobson. "Would you explain?"

89

"Her visit reminded me of Reverend Murchison. He was a priest assistant in the 1960s and the only other minister who ever paid me a visit."

"And how does that lead us to Mr. Barrett?"

"Murchison was a good man, a dedicated and humble minister who put his congregation first. He visited us several times while I recovered from surgery. We had two small children and, with me laid up, it was sometimes difficult."

"And Mr. Barrett..."

"Yes, sorry. The visits would have been late 1963 or early 1964. Shortly after that, Reverend Murchison was shoved out, and a new priest assistant brought in. It happened because Murchison complained about Barrett's behaviour."

Simon sighed with relief. They were finally getting somewhere. "Do you know the basis for Reverend Murchison's complaints?"

"Barrett was far too flamboyant for his role as sexton. He was too forward with young women like my wife, and the way he looked at the teenage girls was scandalous."

"Did he actually assault your wife?"

"Not in a way that was considered assault in those days, but he was always touching women and patting them on their behinds." Jerome paused, shrugging his shoulders. "He got away with it because times were different, and he was a dignitary in the church, but my wife and many others didn't appreciate it. If Maddie was still with us, she'd confirm what I've just said."

"Did you relay these concerns to Reverend Murchison?"

"I might have when he visited me during my recovery, but you needn't take my word for it. The police investigated, and Bartholomew Barrett left shortly after."

"Barrettsport Police or the RCMP?"

"I don't rightly know, but I talked to Chief Connaught, Chief DeWolfe's predecessor, so there must be a report in the station's archives."

After a quick beer-free lunch at the Travellers Inn, Simon returned to the station and headed for the archives. If the old chief investigated Bartholomew Barrett's activities, the files would contain the information Simon needed to determine if he should include Barrett in his current search.

The thin file, when he found it, suggested the investigation was not as extensive as Jerome Dobson imagined, or that Barrettsport was only a small player in a larger RCMP probe. If so, he should find a cross-reference to the RCMP file. Requesting it would cause a delay, something Simon wanted to avoid because he yearned to return to his assessment of Alexander Merrick.

He took the file to his office and spread the contents on his desk. The investigation's central focus was immediately evident. They had not been investigating sexual indiscretions as Jerome Dobson had implied, or activities of a New England ex-patriot who might be related to the original Barrett. Their case focused on fraudulent business dealings. Bartholomew Barrett sold shares in mines and other investments of dubious value to unsuspecting investors. He was basically the mid-twentieth-century equivalent of the Victorian era snake oil salesman.

An advertisement clipped from the Halifax Mail Star explained the link to the church. He featured his role as sexton in St George's Church prominently. Simon now understood Bartholomew carefully cultivated the minister and other important people in the church, inveigling himself into their good graces. His appointment as sexton gave him *gravitas* he could use to convince naïve and unsuspecting punters to buy the worthless gold mine shares he hawked.

Other documents in the file indicated a long history as a salesman of dubious goods. He'd arrived in Nova Scotia and settled in Barrettsport after Ontario became too hot for him. Biographical details in the file did not eliminate him as a possible father for the baby or prove he didn't have another role in the disposal of the child. But an incestuous relationship seemed unlikely, and the picture didn't fit the one Simon had developed for the child's father. Bartholomew Barrett was an unscrupulous salesman, all bluster and superficial knowledge, not the meticulous and obsessive perfectionist who orchestrated placement of the body in the sacristy.

Simon summarized his knowledge of Bartholomew Barrett, added those notes to his file for unlikely, but not impossible suspects, and returned to his expanding file on Alexander Merrick.

91

Chapter Nineteen

Friday morning, Simon failed to convince Chief DeWolfe they should focus on Alexander Merrick. His request for a DNA sample from Mayor Merrick also fell on deaf ears.

The chief was adamant. "I will not authorize a request for Mayor Merrick's DNA sample. We cannot pester the mayor or any of his family members until you have better grounds."

"But why not? A simple test would end thoughts of Alexander's involvement if the DNA sample clears the family. John Rice volunteered a sample that cleared his family, and others have been willing."

"Perhaps he would, but you cannot solve this by asking everyone to provide a DNA sample. For one thing we can't afford the cost, and second, it infringes on everyone's rights. Follow proper procedure. Find evidence pointing toward an identity for the baby, and then I'll agree to the DNA samples."

Simon shook his head, annoyed at the implied criticism. "I'll get back to my list of potential parents, but Alexander Merrick is on it."

"I'm not dissuading you from following that lead, but don't ignore your others. I won't have you focussing on one suspect and ignoring leads that take you in other directions."

"Yes, sir. I'll keep you informed."

Not the greatest situation, Simon thought as he returned to his office. A simple request would quickly establish Alexander Merrick's involvement one way or the other.

The cost of a single DNA analyses was trivial, and a request for a voluntary sample infringed on no one's rights. So, why was Chief

DeWolfe generating roadblocks? If he was withholding information critical to Simon's case, it would leave him in an untenable situation.

More likely, he was protecting the family patriarchs from incursions into their lives without actually knowing they were hiding anything. The poolside antics Simon had observed at the summer garden parties indicated Nicole and other family members felt they responded to a different moral authority than the normal citizens. Chief DeWolfe often complained that the families expected and received preferential treatment from the police. Simon feared the families 'we are above the law' attitude would become an issue as the case proceeded. He could only hope the chief was a victim of the families' behaviour, not a co-conspirator.

Simon spent the next few hours tracking down Alexander Merrick's aunt. He found her living with her husband in Bridgewater and drove to interview them.

"And you think I could have been the child's mother?" Eleanor Boudreau asked after Simon explained the reason for his visit.

"I'm simply trying to eliminate possibilities."

"And I might be a possibility because I had a falling out with my family and married Henri?"

"We're accusing no one, but we were uncertain about your activities in 1961 and 1962, the exact period we're focusing on."

"At one time, your comments would have made me very sad or very angry, but now, so many years later, I feel I should just laugh." She paused and looked at her husband. "I'd rather you told him while I make tea."

Henri Boudreau waited until he heard Eleanor filling the kettle. "So long ago, but it still makes us sad." He paused, took a deep breath and launched into his explanation. "Eleanor cannot bear a child. We spent months during the years you're interested in visiting hospitals and clinics in Ontario and the United States looking for a miracle, but there was none. The baby you found can't be hers."

Simon may have eliminated Aunt Eleanor, but he refused to give up on Alexander Merrick. Merrick's character fit too perfectly with Simon's mental picture of the person responsible. He'd failed to establish a link between Alexander and a woman with the right genetic makeup, but Simon refused to eliminate him.

93

By Friday evening, Simon had an address for Merrick in a Halifax suburb. He decided to combine his ongoing investigation with a visit with Brian Curtis, his wife, Josie, and their two girls. Brian was a friend from his days training in the Police Academy in British Columbia who was now on the Halifax police force. Prior to befriending Nicole Adams and Josh Corkum, Brian was Simon's only friend in Nova Scotia. He spent Saturday afternoon with Nicole and Josh, and Sunday he travelled to Halifax for dinner with Brian and his family.

In Halifax, Simon detoured to the address he'd found for Alexander Merrick. Merrick's small house in a run-down suburb was freshly painted and generally well maintained with colourful flowers around the foundation. The lawn was overgrown but not particularly unkempt, with no sign of the rusting cars and trailers dominating many yards.

"Is Mr. Merrick around?" Simon asked a neighbour raking debris in his yard.

He replied without looking up from his task. "Haven't seen him for several weeks."

"Is that normal? The lawn's overgrown and the plants in the front window need watering."

"No idea. I really don't know him." The man stopped working and leaned on his rake. "He's a cantankerous old sod, and I avoid him as much as possible. I hope he never comes back, but I will miss his sister. She's a nice friendly woman who shares anything she has with everyone. Not very bright, a mongoloid, but we're not supposed to call them that any longer. She'll be unhappy when she sees her plants."

Sister. Down's syndrome. Alexander's sister had resurfaced. Simon's mind whirled with new questions and a new relationship to consider.

"What about other neighbours?" he asked, mostly to fill in time while he processed the new revelation. "Would one have a key and perhaps go in to water the plants?"

"I doubt it. He's on good terms with no one."

"What about the sister? You say she has Down's syndrome."

"Yeah, that's what you're supposed to call it. He said she was his sister, but she must be twenty years younger than he is. Despite my general opinion of him, I must admit he is good to her. He causes his neighbours endless grief, but he's good to the poor woman."

"How long have they lived here?"

"They were here when we moved in twelve years ago. One old neighbour, he's no longer with us, said Merrick had a wife. But that was before my time."

94

"Do you know the wife's name or what happened to her?"

The man shook his head. "All I know is she hasn't lived there during the last twelve years."

"And you have no idea when Merrick might return?"

"Sorry, no idea."

Simon had a new focus as he drove from Merrick's house to supper with Brian Curtis and family. Alexander Merrick's neighbour had reminded him of a player he'd ignored—Merrick's sister, the one with Down's syndrome. She had not died as Nicole Adams suggested but had been living with Alexander for more than a decade. Could she be the baby's mother?

Chapter Twenty

Before Simon left Halifax, Brian Curtis promised to consult the patrol cops in Alexander Merrick's neighbourhood and relay any observations they made. The call arrived less than four days later on Thursday morning. The interruption was welcome. Simon had made little progress searching for information on Alexander Merrick's time in the Halifax suburb, his purported wife, or his sister Felicity.

Brian sounded breathless. "Simon, someone's broken into Merrick's abandoned house. You need to see this."

"What's the hurry?"

"There's a message. It could be important."

"Oh?"

"The interior walls are covered with signal flags. They may be sending a message related to your investigation. My constable will record the sequences, but you should see it in person."

"Is this a joke?" Simon asked, holding his phone at arm's length while he allowed himself a quiet chuckle. Brian loved pranks. If this was a joke, he'd call it off soon enough.

"I'm serious. It sounds like something from a Hardy Boys book, but this is real. The walls are literally covered with signal flags. They might be sending you an important message. Check out the video clip I emailed you."

Brian's tone and the cell phone video he transmitted proved he wasn't joking. "I'm on my way," Simon announced.

"Bring a change of clothes. You can stay at our place while you investigate."

From early May until the last week of June, Simon had been stumbling around delving into ancient history. Then, over the next ten days, several potential parents were eliminated. When he learned on July seventh that Alexander Merrick and Felicity were living in the house in Halifax, he had a clear reason to focus on his prime suspect. Now, four days later, Brian Curtis claimed he'd uncovered an important new lead.

"What do you have for me?" Simon asked three hours later as he strode toward Brian standing in the doorway of Alexander Merrick's house.

"Small house, well cared for, occupied by a man and a woman using separate bedrooms. All records, books, papers, computers, *et cetera* have been removed, and everything from the woman's room. Clothes remain in the man's room and no obvious gaps where furniture's missing. Listed owner is your Alexander Merrick. The neighbours say no one's been here since mid-June."

"What were you telling me about signal flags?"

Brian turned and marched inside. "The walls are covered with international maritime signal flags sewn from simple cloth that looks like cotton. I'm no sewing expert, but they don't look like professionally made flags."

"I see what you mean," Simon replied, staring at the living room walls. They were covered from floor to ceiling with flags with no spaces between them. Starting at the top left-hand corner of the wall they faced, Simon saw a square with black, yellow, blue and red triangles radiating from a central point. This was followed by a red diamond on a white background, another with black, yellow, blue and red triangles, then a yellow cross on a red field. Eight more equally colourful flags completed the top row.

The cream coloured wall showed where the flags didn't quite reach the window frame. Additional patches of wall were visible behind white and blue flags with a notch cut out of one side. Other walls had similarly shaped red ones. The room was a cacophony of red, white, blue, yellow and black patches of various shapes and sizes.

Simon shook his head in disbelief. "Your photographer won't do justice to this scene."

"This isn't a major crime scene, so I can't engage the forensics unit. We've photographed the walls, and my constable's recording the sequence of letters and numbers."

"You're telling me these are signal flags ships used in bygone eras, and there's one for each letter and number?"

97

"I thought you participated in sailboat races back in Vancouver. Sailors should be familiar with signal flags; they're used by the race organizers to send messages to the boats."

"I'm not much of a sailor. Mostly, I helped keep the damned thing upright. If I remember correctly, they raised a white flag ten minutes before the race started, then a blue one at five minutes and a red one at the start. There were other flags flying from the committee boat, but I never paid attention to them."

Someone called from the back of the house, and Brian disappeared. Simon stared at the flags, thinking about his days sailing on Vancouver's English Bay. He was a novice sailor but more interested than he'd implied. Barrettsport had a beautiful harbour. The image he'd generated several days ago of his own sailboat popped back into his head.

Brian returned and resumed their conversation. "Fortunately, Bill Walker, my constable, is a more experienced sailor. He immediately recognized what they were. Merrick may have used them to send a message, a confession of some sort or instructions re his whereabouts. But I should warn you, Bill sometimes goes overboard when it comes to codes. He's seen messages where none exist. This time I'm inclined to give him some encouragement. It could be a message."

"So, what will you do?"

"Bill will finish recording the complete sequence, and then I'll give him an opportunity to decode it. If he succeeds, we'll send you the results. It might take considerable effort because there's no distinction between capitals and lower-case letters, no punctuation, and whoever did this didn't put spaces between the words. The letters run together in one long string."

"It goes around this room, and the next one," Simon said pointing into the dining room. "What about the rest of the house?"

"These two rooms have completely covered walls and one room upstairs, his bedroom, has a partial row."

"So, where's your constable?"

"Upstairs in the bedroom. He should soon have the message, or whatever it is, recorded."

Simon peered at the nearest flag. He lifted one corner and inspected a seam. Simon was no expert, but the seams looked pretty good to him. The lines of thread were straight and the stitches evenly spaced.

He turned to Brian. "You said they aren't professionally made?"

Brian laughed. "If you were married and had a wife who's as fussy about sewing as Josie is, you'd know. Believe me, they're homemade and

98

not up to Josie's standards. Upstairs in the smaller bedroom, we found an empty table and strands of thread on the floor. I assume she made them using a sewing machine that's been removed."

"Would someone with Down's syndrome be capable of sewing these? They may not be professionally done, but it would take manual dexterity and some intelligence."

"People with Down's syndrome aren't completely incapable. Many accomplish lots of things. They're not nearly as helpless as people think."

Simon sighed, thinking about the extra research he'd be conducting. "What about financial records or paper that gives us a hint about where they've gone?"

"I already said there isn't anything. It was cleaned up and either destroyed or taken away. And we have no search warrant."

"We could legitimately search for information that would help locate them, and tell them about the break-in."

"There's nothing, so the point is moot."

"Phone messages?"

"No phone and no answering machine. He may have a cell."

Simon strolled through the dining room to the kitchen where a constable was repairing the back door. He wondered if Brian would object if he snooped around a Halifax Police Department crime scene but decided against it. Brian or one of the constables would have discovered anything useful.

He returned to the living room. "Okay, what's your plan?"

"When Bill finishes recording the signal flag message, we'll get the damage to the back door repaired, and he'll try to locate Mr. Merrick. We'll make sure you receive Bill's transcription of the message and a complete photographic record. That's about it." He paused, glancing around the room. "As far as the Halifax force is concerned, this is a simple break-in."

"Thank you for temporarily treating it as more than a break-in. It could be a major development for my investigation."

Brian thumped Simon's back. "We do what we can to help our fellow officers. If all's well with Bill, we can return to my place, and you can entertain our tykes until he provides us with the finished transcript."

Bill Wagner arrived at Brian's apartment in the evening when Josie was busy putting Jessica and Kathryn to bed.

99

"I've locked the house, made copies of the photos for Detective Goodyear, and passed the case back to the people who deal with break-ins. I've also transcribed the message, including four flags I didn't recognize. They're shown as asterisks, and I've drawn pictures of the unknown flags at the bottom."

"Could they be numbers or other specialized flags?" Brian asked his constable.

Bill shook his head. "The numbers, repeaters, and other specialized flags are triangular pennants, and the colour schemes are wrong."

After a glance, Brian passed the pages to Simon. "Here are the raw data."

Simon perused the sheets of paper. They were copies of pages from the constable's notebook. The entries comprised strings of seemingly meaningless letters.

The first page had 'living room, south-facing wall' at the top followed by 'naqrenqn-vpvgljnf-ubzrsbeu-verfphrq-ybbxrqns-a****jur-uzlfvfgrenaqfu-regvzrpnzrvqryvi'.

The next page had 'living room, west facing wall' followed by 'zfzreevpxnaq-avarjurazlsn-naqvpnccrqcr-ures-greu-avun-rorp-rerq'.

Then 'living room, north facing wall' and 'vunirfvaarqzlfvf-gureonaavfurq-bcyrgjblrnefy-ebzgurubzrna-rerirefvaprvf-qpneanyeryngv-nzrcertana-bheonoltveyjv'; then 'living room, east facing wall' followed by 'zlanzrvfnyrk-gresry-uregbn-ngre-qvunir-vaarqv-bafjvg-gjurau'.

The entries for the dining room began with the south facing wall and 'gubhgceboyr-qjurafur-fbyqfurj-nlnaqwh-vvagreer-zonyzvat-uhepuva-puhepugu'.

Next was the west wall and 'znaq-jnfb-ragg-fgqv-qgur-vafgtrbetr-oneerggfcb-ngunqjrypb'.

The north facing wall with 'jranzrqureu-aylf-bfyr-qabg-obql-fnat-eggu-zrqz', and the east facing wall with 'bcrubcrqvr-vkjrrx-rcbarq-jnxrhc-nsgrer-yvpnac-rbayl-rfurvf' finished that room.

Finally, there was one entry for an upstairs bedroom, only ten letters across the top of the wall with the doorway. They were 'erfgvatcrn'.

"These are transcriptions for each wall starting in the upper left-hand corner with the ends of the rows indicated by a hyphen," Bill offered without prompting.

"But are you convinced it's a message?" Brian asked.

"It has to be a coded message. I'd like a chance to decipher it if you can spare me for a few hours. I see patterns that should let me break into the code, but it might take some effort."

"Give it a few hours and send me a progress report. If something comes up, we'll pull the plug and pass whatever you have to Simon."

"Thanks, boss, you know I enjoy these puzzles. I'll work on it tonight. I might have an answer by morning."

Brian shook his head as Bill closed the door. "Crazy bugger. He'll spend all night on his damn puzzle and be falling asleep at his desk tomorrow, but he'll find the solution if it's a code."

"Good, because I wouldn't have a clue."

"Neither would I, but enough of that. Time for a beer or two assuming you're staying the night."

"Yeah, sure, if it's not too much trouble for Josie."

"The kids will enjoy it, and you should have a decoded message to take home with you tomorrow morning."

"So, what are you working on?" Simon asked as Brian placed beer bottles on the coffee table.

Brian gazed toward the bedrooms. He apparently didn't want Josie or the kids listening. "An old case about women vanishing from the streets. We had a number of disappearances, mostly in the 1990s, that haven't been resolved. The investigators were convinced organized crime, possibly human trafficking, was behind them, but nothing was proven."

"These were women in the sex trade?"

"Yeah, young women on the margins of life mostly addicted to drugs, and some were definitely sex trade workers." Brian shrugged his shoulders. "Others, we're not so sure."

"And the case is suddenly hot again?"

"Another young woman disappeared a month ago. Bill and I are trying to link three recent ones with the spate in the mid-'90s. So far with no positive results."

"So, nothing that connects with my problem."

Brian sighed before draining his beer. "Just a few hours helping a friend and colleague."

Friday morning, they found Bill hunched over his police station computer. "You're in too early. I couldn't work on it last night, so I don't have it solved. It doesn't look difficult." He looked up at Simon. "I'll get the answer to you as soon as it's done."

"I should hit the road," Simon said turning to Brian. "I need to inform my chief about yesterday's discovery, and there's nothing more for me here."

"If you must. But you're welcome to stay longer."

"I realize that, but it's time I reciprocated. The four of you should make an effort to visit Barrettsport sometime soon. Summer's here, we can take the kids to the beach."

Brian laughed. "And if you buy a few more plates, we can even stay for dinner."

"The decoded message will be on your computer before you arrive home," Bill promised as Simon took his leave. He didn't respond to Brian's crack about plates, but his friend had a point, Simon's apartment was sparsely furnished.

Chapter Twenty-One

Simon arrived at his office after the two-hour trip from Halifax and immediately checked his email. The copied message from Bill Walker to Brian Curtis contained the solution to the flag puzzle.

The puzzle is solved. No challenge whatsoever, just a simple displacement problem, a Caesar cipher: frequencies of various letters fit the usual pattern and instances of repeated letters and other common sequences are, with a few exceptions, consistent with normal English usage. Decoded letter sequence for each wall is attached. I can't immediately pick out the message. Simon will know the context, he should sort it out. Bill

The attachment read:

Living Room South: anderada-icitywas-homeforh-irescued-lookedaf-n****whe-hmysisterandsh-ertimecameideliv

West: msmerrickand-ninewhenmyfa-andicappedpe-herf-terh-niha-ebec-ered

North: ihavesinnedmysis-therbannished-opletwoyearsl-romthehomean-ereversinceis-dcarnalrelati-amepregnan-ourbabygirlwi

East: mynameisalex-terfel-hertoa-ater-dihave-innedi-onswit-twhenh

Dining Room south: thoutproble-dwhenshe-soldshew-ayandju-iinterre-mbalming-hurchin/-churchth

West: mand-waso-entt-stdi-dthe-instgeorge-barrettspo-athadwelco

North: wenamedherh-nlys-osle-dnot-body-sang-rtth-medm

East: opehopedie-ixweek-eponed-wakeup-aftere-licanc-eonly-esheis

Bedroom: restingpea

When the answer wasn't immediately obvious, Simon returned to square one. He looked up Caesar cipher in Wikipedia and learned that it was, as Bill said, a simple displacement code where each letter is replaced by the one that falls thirteen letters later in the alphabet. This meant the message could be decoded by reapplying the cipher. But knowing the definition didn't get him further ahead.

Next, he searched for the identity of the four mystery flags. Again, the answer was readily available on the web. They were flags used in the United States for the numbers one, nine, six and four. Apparently, the letter flags were universal, but different countries used different flags for the numbers and other ancillary tasks. The chosen convention suggested a link with the United States that Simon couldn't immediately understand.

One, nine, six, four was probably a year. Replacing the four asterisks with 1964 suggested the short line 'n1964whe' could be 'in 1964 when'. But the 'i' and 'n' were not in the rows immediately above and below.

After staring for a while, Simon decided the single line in the upstairs bedroom held the key. It suggested, as Bill had obviously already concluded, that the message started at the top left-hand corner of a wall. That gave eight possibilities for the start—the top lines on each of the downstairs walls—'Anderada', Msmerrrickand', 'Ihavesinnedmysis', 'Mynameisalex', 'Thoutproble', 'Mand', 'Wenamedherh', and 'Opehopedie'. He discounted the first, second, fifth, and eighth possibility. He couldn't turn the beginnings of those letter combinations into meaningful words that might have started a sentence. The sixth was too short to conclude anything, but the third, fourth and seventh looked promising. Three could easily be 'I have sinned my sis'. Four and seven could be 'My name is Alex', and 'We named her H'. From these possibilities, 'My name is Alex…' seemed like the best bet for the beginning of a message.

Diana Jackson appeared in his office doorway, interrupting Simon's train of thought. "Time for a coffee break?"

"Sure, why not?" he replied, waving her into his office.

She placed two cups of steaming coffee on his desk and leaned over perusing the scraps of paper with the letter sequences. "Looks like you're working on a mysterious code like the kids in an Enid Blyton story."

"How did you reach that conclusion so quickly?"

"No special insight," Diana said, smiling, "Margaret told me you came in with a book about codes."

Simon laughed, holding up a book after rummaging around his desk top. "Library book from the children's section. This might look like

104

something from A Fabulous Five mystery, but it's serious. I suspect it's the key to the identity of my body."

"The *Famous* Five," Diana replied, placing emphasis on the word famous. "I read them all when I was growing up. Can I help with your schoolboy coded message mystery?"

He explained where he stood, and she transposed the first few words 'My name is Alex' to his freshly cleaned whiteboard.

Simon drummed his fingers on his desk. "If I have this right, the message starts at the top left-hand corner of the east-facing wall, but then where did he go?"

"Not to the next row?"

"That's how Bill was thinking when he recorded the message. He treated the walls like pages in a book."

"But this isn't a book, they're rooms in a house," Diana pointed out. "The message could go around the room on the top row before repeating with the second row and so on."

"If that's correct, and we have the right starting point, the rest of the top row becomes a n d e r a d a m s m e r r i c k a n d i h a v e s i n n e d m y s i and s."

Diana added the letters to the board as Simon read them off. She inserted spaces between possible words and a little punctuation to produce 'My name is Alexander Adams Merrick and I have sinned. My sis...'

"Now we're getting somewhere," Simon exclaimed. "The first three letters of the second row are 'ter' which completes the word sister."

After a phone call that briefly broke his concentration, Simon confirmed Alexander Merrick's middle name was, in fact, Adams. When he looked up from his computer, Diana had the whole message transcribed to his whiteboard in her very careful and precise handwriting. It was much neater than anything he would have produced.

The message read:

My name is Alexander Adams Merrick, and I have sinned. My sister Felicity was nine when my father banished her to a home for mentally handicapped people. Two years later I rescued her from the home, and I have looked after her ever since. I sinned in 1964 when I had carnal relations with my sister and she became pregnant. When her time came, I delivered our baby girl without problem and we named her Hope. Hope died when she was only six weeks old. She went to sleep one day and just did not wake up. I interred the body after embalming in the St. George's Anglican Church in Barrettsport, the only church that had welcomed me. She is resting pea...

105

Simon smiled when he finished reading the message. "That's it—case solved. Let's go to the Traveller's Inn for lunch and a celebratory drink. It's on me."

"Sorry," Diana replied, returning to the desk and picking up her mostly full coffee cup. "You forget, I'm a lowly constable on shift until four. I can't go traipsing off to lunch."

A solitary lunch wasn't ideal for celebration, and Simon started enumerating the remaining loose ends, and the possible pitfalls he hadn't considered. By the time he finished eating, he had a sizable list:

1. At the time Alexander said the home released Felicity into his care, she would have been eleven. Would they have released her without his father's consent?

2. How much did Alexander's father know, and why was Richard Merrick apparently so badly informed?

Simon underlined why was Richard Merrick apparently so badly informed. Could the mayor be hiding important information about his two siblings? He shook his head and continued.

3. Can a woman with Down's syndrome bear a child and if she did, would the baby's DNA show the mother had the syndrome?

4. Would the baby have Down's syndrome?

5. Could Alexander and Felicity live together for forty-five years without it coming to someone's attention?

6. Why did Alexander make this confession, and why now?

7. Could Alexander have orchestrated the break-in to draw attention to his message?

8. Could the whole flag episode be a perverted joke or an indication Alexander had cracked up?

9. Where were Alexander and Felicity?

Simon returned to his office wondering how he should express progress to the chief. He had to relay the content of the message he and Diana deciphered. It gave them a credible answer to the question he was officially investigating, namely the identity of the baby; It also provided identities for her two parents and an explanation of how she died. He could then point out that he needed to find Alexander and Felicity Merrick and obtain DNA samples. That would unequivocally prove the baby's lineage and his job would be done.

106

None of the concerns he'd identified at lunch would matter if DNA evidence proved Alexander and Felicity were the parents, so probably best not to mention them. It would then be the church's job to bring closure to the infant's brief and tragic life. And the prosecutor's office could decide what, if anything, they should do about charging anyone with a crime.

It all happened so many years earlier. Quite possibly the only crimes committed were a failure to inform the proper authorities about the birth and death of a child, and the illegal disposal of human remains. The actual death could have been by natural causes as described in the message, and the likelihood of proving otherwise, very remote.

The chief arrived at one forty-five, listened to Simon's account and immediately called the mayor. At five past two, they were in Mayor Merrick's office, and Simon was repeating his story.

"So, sir, that's the situation," Simon concluded after a ten-minute spiel during which neither the chief nor the mayor interrupted him. "We must find your brother and sister to get DNA samples to confirm everything. Then it will no longer be a police matter."

"If I provided a DNA sample, would that answer the question?" Mayor Merrick asked.

"I'm no expert, but I think it would be helpful, but not definitive."

"I would happily provide one, but I have something to show you. If you're up for a short stroll, you should follow me."

The mayor said no more but rose, fetched his hat, and exited his office obviously expecting Simon and the chief to follow. He stopped briefly to consult with his secretary, then led the way onto Second Avenue and out toward the large estates on the point. He talked about several civic projects he was pursuing but provided no insight into their immediate quest. Simon soon realized they were headed for the mayor's house across Shore Road from the large estates.

Chapter Twenty-Two

The mayor's housekeeper met them at his front door.

"Sorry for the unexpected intrusion, Mrs. Morrison, but I have business with the chief and Detective Goodyear. Would you prepare coffee and something for Felicity?"

Simon stumbled over the top step when he heard her name mentioned. He'd wondered why the mayor escorted them to his house. Finding the mayor's younger sister on the premises was not one of the possibilities he'd imagined. "Felicity! Do you mean your sister?" he exclaimed as he struggled to regain his balance and his composure.

The mayor laughed at the ruse he'd generated. "Caught you by surprise, didn't I? Felicity has indeed surfaced. Meeting her should be the way to start a discussion that's imperative."

He led the way up a large formal staircase to a bright, lavishly furnished bedroom. A short, somewhat overweight woman with a round face and thick glasses hunched over a sewing machine.

"It's stopped working again," she said when she noticed Mayor Merrick in the doorway. An impediment made her slur her esses, but her speech was understandable.

"I'll fix it for you," he replied. "But first I want you to meet two of my friends."

"Okay." She stood and walked, smiling broadly, to the door. No sign of reluctance or insecurity, thought Simon.

"This is Reginald, he's the policemen's boss, and Simon, one of his policemen."

"Where is your uniform?" she asked Simon before taking his hand and leading him over to her sewing table. "Policemen are supposed to wear uniforms, so I will recognize them if I need help."

"But some policemen don't wear uniforms, and I'm one of them. You must remember what I look like."

"Do you like my sewing machine? I use it to make flags, a different flag for each letter. There are twenty-six letters, and each one has its own flag. And special flags for the numbers."

"I did know that and also that you like making flags."

"It's my favourite thing. If you tell me the letter for your name, I could find a flag for you."

"Would you? That would be great. My name's Simon," he said emphasizing the ess sound. "It starts with an ess."

She sorted through a pile of flags and produced a white flag with a blue square in its centre.

"This is an ess, and it's for you," she said, presenting him with the flag.

"Really, for me? Why thank you," Simon replied, bowing as he accepted the gift. "I'll put it on the wall in my office at the police station, and when you visit, you can see it."

"Do you have chocklit at the police station? I 'specially like chocklit when I go visiting." She turned to her brother. "Can we have chocklit now?"

"Why don't we see if Mrs. Morrison can find you some hot chocolate, but Simon, Reginald and I will have coffee instead."

"But I don't like coffee."

"That's okay, you'll learn Mrs. Morrison is already making your hot chocolate."

"Mrs. Morrison," she yelled, hurrying from the room, "Richard says I can have chocklit."

The mayor watched her charge down the stairs before turning to his visitors. He motioned for them to follow as he also, albeit more slowly, descended the staircase.

"It's been a joy having her with us for the last few weeks. She's like a little girl in many ways, but completely reliable and capable of looking after herself, so she's been no trouble." He paused at the foot of the staircase. "I wonder what we'll do with the signal flags she's sewing? She obviously feels they're her big responsibility in life. I had no idea why until you told me about Alexander's house."

109

"That part seems clear," Simon replied, "but you must explain how Felicity resurfaced."

"In a minute. She won't stay after Janice pours her chocolate, and then we can talk."

Felicity perched on a kitchen stool swinging her legs back and forth like a child. She watched Janice Morrison pour the hot liquid into her mug and took one look at the steam rising from it.

"It's too hot, I'll come back." She jumped down from the counter. "I'm going to find kitty."

The chief watched Felicity disappear in search of the cat. "Do you need clarification on anything we described in your office?"

Mayor Merrick shook his head. "I should start. Then no one can accuse me of fabricating a story to fit what you already know."

"All right, go ahead."

"I should begin in 1958 when I was ten and Felicity two years younger. My father decided she would be better off in a facility equipped to provide her with professional help and companionship of others like herself. Alexander was twenty-one or twenty-two and wouldn't accept the decision. It caused a big row, and he left home never to return. I suspect you've discovered most of this, but it sets the stage."

Simon nodded. "We'd pieced that together."

"My father funded the long-term care facility with the expectation they'd care for Felicity until she died. He didn't want Alexander or me or anyone else to be responsible for Felicity. No one talked about her, and I accepted she'd passed away many years ago. Then, three weeks ago, the facility manager told me Alexander had been looking after Felicity for years. He'd returned her to the home with instructions to contact me if they needed to communicate with the family."

"Did they explain why he did this?" Simon asked.

"Apparently, Alexander returned her for short periods when he had to go into a hospital or had another reason he couldn't look after her. They concluded he was ill again. Alexander is much older than Felicity or me, in his late seventies."

"We're aware of his age, but is there proof he's ill?"

"I don't think so." Mayor Merrick paused and tilted his head to the side, pursing his lips. Simon wondered what he was pondering, but the mayor chose not to elaborate. "After learning Felicity was alive and well, we had a discussion here in the family and decided we should invite her to live with us. I collected her and her stuff two weeks ago."

110

"Her possessions included her sewing machine and clothes, anything else?"

"Nothing except a lot of cloth and thread and other stuff related to her sewing, and a stack of signal flags."

"So that's the story." The chief turned to Simon while drumming his fingers on the counter. "Anything to add?"

"Only that we suspect Alexander told her which flags he wanted one letter at a time. Does she ask you what letters to sew?"

The mayor nodded but looked puzzled. "What about the baby? Are you sure it's their baby, and would she even remember her?"

Much to Simon's relief, the chief made the necessary request. "Alexander's confession says it's her baby, but DNA evidence will prove it without doubt, so we do need a DNA sample from Felicity. For what she remembers, you must consult the medics."

"They won't know any better than we would," Mayor Merrick said. "But what happens now?"

"Talk to the minister about a burial service for the child," the chief suggested.

"And we still want to find Alexander," Simon added. "Please, tell us if you have any idea where he may be."

"That's easy," Mayor Merrick responded as Felicity returned to drink her no longer too hot chocolate. "I haven't seen the fellow for forty years. No idea where he could be."

"So, you were a teenager when you last met," Simon continued. "And no communication since?"

"That's right. I don't think anyone has seen him since 1965, but there were two people, rather disreputable looking men, asking about him in the nineties. Don't you remember Chief, I'm sure it was reported?"

"It does remind me," the chief said. "We were told about them. We assumed they were trying to collect on a debt, but we never encountered them."

"The other thing that concerns me," Simon said to Mayor Merrick while watching the chief to gauge his reaction, "is your father's role. The home wouldn't release Felicity into Alexander's care unless your father agreed. So, if you can find any records that shed light on your father's role, I would like to see them."

"That's hardly relevant," interjected the chief, "unless George Merrick was somehow involved in the baby's death. It's not anything we should pursue."

111

Simon shrugged his shoulder and let the matter be. It was possible George Merrick, not Alexander Merrick, was the father, and someone, Richard or George's lawyers perhaps, might be sitting on relevant information.

Simon addressed the chief as they walked to the station. "I know where to find Alexander."

"Where might he be?"

"At a religious retreat, something like the Anglican monastery Reverend McKnight retired to in the 1960s. I should start my search at that very place, and if I don't find him there, extend it to other religious retreats."

"I suppose it fits with his penchant for theological dialogue, but I'm not sure finding him should be a priority. The prosecutor's office, however, may have a different opinion."

Simon stopped to hold open the station's main door. He followed the chief into the station. "Probably not, given the uncertainty in the coroner's determination on the cause of death. But we shouldn't ignore the failure to report the death and disposal of the body."

"It's no longer our problem. We should see the baby is finally put to rest, make Felicity as welcome as possible now she's back home, and close the file."

"I can start by mounting my signal flag on my office wall, and we can make sure our canteen has cocoa available when she comes to visit."

"We can ask her to make flags for everyone in the office," Chief DeWolfe added. "That should keep her busy."

The chief disappeared into his office clearly happy an annoying case had been solved, but Simon was less sure. He wouldn't be happy until he had DNA results that confirmed the baby's lineage.

Chapter Twenty-Three

A Monday morning phone call from the laboratory analyzing Richard and Felicity Merrick's DNA samples destroyed their explanation of the baby's parentage.

The lab analyst came straight to the point. "The samples you submitted last week show neither of these individuals is a parent of your baby."

Simon snorted. DNA evidence appeared to upset the applecart every time he made progress. But this time, he was neither disappointed nor surprised. The surreal scene at Alexander Merrick's house never rang true.

"Can you say that with certainty?" he asked.

"Degradation of the DNA samples we retrieved from the baby concerns us, but we can say with a high level of confidence all three are closely related. The new samples, however, are not the parents. The statistical details are in the report."

"What do you mean by closely related? Siblings, uncle and aunt, or cousins?"

"Details are in the report we'll email, but, basically, you're on the right track."

Simon terminated the call and immediately typed a text message to Chief DeWolfe. If Felicity was not the mother, they must postpone funeral arrangements. Next, he called Brian Curtis to ensure the hair samples collected at Alexander Merrick's house were analyzed. They didn't provide an indisputable link to Merrick, so they wouldn't be admissible in court, but Simon needed to confirm Alexander was the father. Those samples were his best bet.

After talking to Brian, Simon sought the chief's okay to contact Mayor Merrick.

"If we ignore the scientific waffle words, they're saying Felicity is not the mother," Richard Merrick said after Simon broke the news.

"And you're not the father," Simon added.

The mayor snorted. "That's not news, but it begs the question, what happens now?"

"We keep looking for the parents, and I could use your help if you're willing."

"Fine, now we have Felicity home with us, we want to help. But what about the memorial service?"

"That's not my decision, but given the renewed uncertainty about the parental identity, you may want to delay."

Mayor Merrick sighed. They were talking on the phone, so Simon couldn't see the mayor's reaction. The audible sigh suggested he wasn't enthusiastic about new twists in the saga. "No real choice. Meanwhile, what do you need from me?"

"First, contact the long-term care facility and get copies of whatever records they have. I'm interested in arrangements for her release into Alexander's care, dates and duration of times she returned to the facility. Anything you can find."

"Will they give me such information?"

"They should since you're now her guardian, and if they won't we'll get a court order."

"Anything else?"

Simon hesitated before answering. The mayor's helpful attitude was a new twist in his relationship with the families. He wasn't sure how far he should push. "Two more things. First, do you have records explaining your father's role?"

"I can answer that. I do not."

"Okay, but the family law firm might, so you could check there. And finally, take Felicity to your family doctor and ask him or her to determine if Felicity ever bore a child?"

"Why does that matter?"

Simon anticipated the objection. Most observers, including the mayor, would accept the DNA results as reported and move on. But, as part of a police investigation, he needed unequivocal answers.

"It will eliminate the small degree of uncertainty that remains because the fifty-year-old DNA sample isn't perfect."

"What does the chief say?"

"I consulted him before calling you. He agrees we should pursue all three."

"Consider it done. I'll get back to you when I learn anything."

Simon set the phone back in its cradle wondering if the mayor would be forthcoming concerning anything he learned about his father, but what could he do? He was basically on a fishing trip, so he had no mechanism to force the mayor or his lawyers to release information they didn't want to release.

Next, Simon returned to the question plaguing him for weeks. Who were the parents? The DNA results proved the parents were close relatives of Mayor Merrick. The mayor was not the father. That left two choices, Alexander, or their father George Merrick. Richard's mother, Elizabeth Merrick, was an Adams but a closely related male cousin in the Adams family was not a contender unless his mother was a Merrick. Another unacknowledged son was another possibility, but Simon needed to eliminate the more obvious candidates before going down that road.

On the maternal side, no simple choices remained. The DNA evidence excluded Felicity, and her aunt Eleanor Boudreau was infertile. Elizabeth Merrick, Richard and Felicity's mother, would have been over fifty when the baby was conceived, and Richard insisted she had a tubal ligation after Felicity was born. So where was the mother? The remaining possibilities were Elizabeth Merrick's siblings and their daughters, or illegitimate sisters Felicity might have had.

Elizabeth Merrick was either Nicole's great-aunt or great-great-aunt. Nicole insisted Simon had done her a huge favour helping her unite with Josh Corkum. It was time to ask her to return the favour by providing genealogical information on the Adams family.

He visited the church at four, Nicole's normal quitting time.

"Simon! It's been ages since I've seen you," she exclaimed when she saw him.

"Ages? Just two weeks. I'd hardly call that ages."

"Maybe not but I missed our Saturdays exploring the countryside."

"Sorry, I was busy and anyway, aren't you and Josh organizing the grand wedding?"

She shook her head. "He's tied up with the boat they're working on, but we're having dinner together tonight. You want to join us?"

"If you wish, but first there's something you can help me with."

"Something concerning the Merricks and the baby's identity?"

115

Simon hesitated. She should not have known about his latest investigations. Richard Merrick must have talked to someone in the Adams family. So much for keeping things private.

"Yes," he sighed. "And Richard Merrick's mother was an Adams, so we have links to your family."

"You want me to give you a lecture on the Adams family tree?"

"If you don't mind. It would save me digging through the records."

"No problem. I'll bring the family bible when we go for dinner. I'll meet you at the water taxi dock at six and we can discuss genealogy?"

"So where are you and Josh planning to eat?" Simon asked as they stepped onto Second Avenue, and Nicole turned toward her apartment.

"Oh, sorry, should have said. The seafood place in Hunter's Creek."

"The coast road diner?"

"No, the little place on the wharf. It's hardly more than a takeout seafood shack, but the fish are good. The outside area with picnic tables is quite okay in nice summer weather, but I wouldn't sit inside at the few tables crammed into a corner."

"But no karaoke nights," Simon suggested, thinking back to Nicole's performance at the pub.

"No karaoke, but good seafood."

"See you at six."

Two hours later, Simon stood on Barrettsport's public dock by the water taxi. At its scheduled departure time, Simon told Eddie, the skipper, Nicole would arrive any minute. He waited.

Several minutes later, Nicole hurried down the dock and straight onto the boat saying nary a word. She obviously expected them to wait for her, and the skipper seemed comfortable with the idea. Simon shook his head and jumped aboard as Eddie cast off the dock lines and engaged the motor.

"What's the matter?" Nicole asked. "I phoned the boat and told Eddie I'd be a few minutes late. It's not a problem."

Nicole was right. The trip would only take fifteen minutes on a pleasant summer evening. The episode was one more example of Barrettsport's flexibility to accommodate individual needs. Simon wondered if Eddie would hold the boat for anyone. The special service was probably restricted to the families.

Whynacht's Fish and Chips, a real down-to-earth eatery, was only a few steps from the floating dock where the taxi tied up. Simon couldn't

116

imagine members of the Barrettsport families receiving special treatment in this joint.

Josh waited with a pitcher of beer at a wooden picnic table on the wharf beside the little restaurant. He poured the beer and Nicole got down to business.

"Here it is, the family history as recorded in the family Bible," she announced as she extracted sheets of printer paper from her purse. "Daddy didn't think the Bible would be safe in this den of iniquity, so I copied the inside of the front cover where everything's recorded."

She handed pages to Josh and Simon before smoothing the last one onto the table in front of her. The waitress arrived before she said anything else.

"Mussels?" Josh suggested, looking at Simon. He must have already known Nicole's opinion. "Should we start with a basket of mussels? I can think of nothing better for a warm summer evening than mussels and beer. And good company, of course."

"Go for it," Simon replied.

Nicole waited for the waitress to leave before turning to Simon. "These are the ones you're interested in—my grandfather, Broderick Adams, born in 1913; his older sister Elizabeth who was married to George Merrick; and their younger sisters, Mary and Linda."

"How did you know I was interested in that generation?" Simon asked, puzzled once again by the fact she always appeared to be one step ahead of him.

"Easy. You've already scoured the bottom of the pot learning everything you can about anyone born from the 1930s, '40s, and '50s. You must be looking one branch lower on the genealogical tree."

"I didn't think we'd been that obvious in our investigations."

"Hard to keep below the radar when it comes to Nicole's family or any of the others," Josh observed. "Accept it. They'll be keeping a close eye on your progress as you search for the identity of the child."

"What can I tell you?" Nicole asked.

"Relationships and liaisons they may have had."

"Marriages and children are here, but not relationships and liaisons."

"Then let's start with marriages and children," Simon suggested.

Nicole hesitated while the waitress distributed three plates and a basket of mussels. She began after the woman took their orders for fish and chips. "Elizabeth was the oldest. She married George Merrick, and they had three kids."

117

"Yeah, we're well acquainted with them. Any suggestion of anything else regarding your great-aunt Elizabeth?"

"I wouldn't know about anything you're interested in."

"Those stories do get around."

"I haven't heard anything, and before you ask, I don't know stories about my grandfather either."

"All right. Who's next? Mary, one year younger than your grandfather."

Nicole pointed at an entry on the page copied from the Bible. "As you can see, she married James Washburn and had three boys and a girl. They lived in Worcester, Massachusetts."

"Their girl, Joan, was born in 1937. It says she died in 1942."

"That's what it says. The Bible doesn't lie."

"So that leaves Linda born in 1917 but it doesn't show any marriage or children."

Nicole stared at the harbour as the waitress cleared away the mussel shells and replaced them with three plates of fish and chips. She said nothing while half-heartedly picking at her fish. "You should talk to Dad or Granddad. She's the unmentioned one in the family. Something happened in 1938 or 1939. After that, she did war-related work in Halifax or Ottawa. Then nothing, no one mentions her."

Josh must have sensed Nicole's reticence. "Let's talk about something else," he suggested, bringing the discussion of Linda Adams to a conclusion. "The wedding for example."

"So, you've set a date?"

"September," Nicole replied.

They talked about the wedding and the boat Josh was finishing until eight thirty when Simon hustled to catch the water taxi to Barrettsport. Two thoughts festered as he crossed the harbour. First, the families apparently had an odd ability to forget family members who failed to live up to expectations. Richard Merrick had apparently been completely ignorant of anything related to his sister Felicity's life and not much better informed about his brother. Now, he'd learned Nicole had a great aunt whose life was equally enigmatic. Second, he'd learned that Linda Adams, the unmentioned aunt, and George Merrick left Barrettsport for war service in Halifax and Ottawa at nearly the same time.

Chapter Twenty-Four

The next morning, Simon started a file on Linda Adams. He searched birth, marriage, and death records and looked for indications she had a Nova Scotia driving license at any time, or a criminal record. He discovered nothing but the actual record of her birth, something he already knew, and her military history. An extensive search for anecdotal information in the local newspaper yielded nothing useful.

Her military records were interesting. Linda joined the first wave of women admitted to the Royal Canadian Air Force in 1940. She shipped to England in 1941, again in the first group of women deployed overseas. She returned to Canada in 1945 and was demobilized.

He'd just discovered she'd been issued a passport a few months after she returned to civilian life when Nicole swept into his office and plunked herself down in his visitor's chair.

"Shouldn't you be working?" Simon asked.

"Lunch break, and I've come to report on my detecting activities."

"It's barely eleven, isn't that early for lunch?"

"It wasn't busy so Rev. Leslie said I could leave early. I thought if what I've learned was valuable enough you would buy me lunch at Mildred's."

Mildred's was Mildred Wexler's Olde English Tea Shoppe, the most unusual eating establishment in Barrettsport's central core, but not a place Simon had visited. It just seemed too dainty and Victorian for his tastes.

"Tell me what you've learned, and I'll tally up what it's worth."

119

"What! That's not very gallant. You're supposed to say 'Of course I'll take you to lunch. It goes without saying and matters not what information you have for me'."

"So, why should I say it?"

She gave him a withering glare. "Because that's the way it's done in proper society. But, seriously, I talked to my grandfather this morning, and he told me about great-aunt Linda."

"I'm ready with my value-added meter. It will tell me if it's enough to justify lunch."

"Simon, behave. He said most kids, that means most of the family's kids, went away to school. Linda was no different. Then Dalhousie University for three years, but she dropped out in 1938."

"Okay, that's interesting. What happened after she dropped out?"

"It gets confusing. I don't know what happened, and Granddad became less than forthcoming. Something happened but he couldn't, or wouldn't, say."

Simon watched her almost bouncing out of her chair as she relayed her information. She was clearly proud of her efforts. "1938?" he asked.

"Yes, 1938. Then he jumped to 1940 when she joined the Air Force. I mean did you know they actually had women in the Air Force in the war? Did they get to fly fighters and other exciting things?"

"I doubt it. Probably stuck on the ground doing clerical work or other mundane activities they needed to make the war machine function."

"Too bad, but I suspect you're right. Granddad said she only stayed in Canada long enough after VE Day to arrange the paperwork to leave again. She returned to England and hasn't been heard from since."

"Okay!" Simon exclaimed, jumping from his chair. Nicole had confirmed suspicions he'd developed after dinner the previous night. A celebration was in order and he was willing to provide the enthusiasm she expected. "What you've told me about unexplained activities in 1938 and leaving Canada never to return in 1945 is well worth the cost of lunch. What is it, the Tea Shoppe or somewhere else?"

"The Tea Shoppe because it's a good place for lunch, and I must return to work."

After a more robust lunch than he expected at a dainty English tea shop, Simon returned to investigate the 1938 to 1940 period in Linda Adams's life. Dalhousie University Registrar's Office confirmed she'd been an undergraduate student from 1936 to 1938, then missed a year before completing her studies in the 1939/40 school year. She graduated in May 1940 with a Bachelor of Arts degree.

Next, he turned to her passport. The 1945 document was not renewed, and no other Canadian passports were issued to Linda Adams. Simon found no records suggesting she resided in Canada after the end of 1945.

Simon shifted his attention to the United Kingdom. He began his search using the extensive publicly accessible websites for births, marriages, and deaths in England. After determining that a Linda M. Adams had married in 1946 and subsequently had three children, he passed the problem to colleagues in England. They would establish whether or not this was the correct Linda Adams and fill in the details.

"Her life is adequately documented except for the summer of 1938 to August 1939 period," Simon informed Diana when she dropped into his office for one of the visits with coffee and cookies that were becoming part of their routine.

She tapped his desk with the stick she'd used to stir milk into her coffee. "Should I dig into her activities during that year?"

"You think she had a baby, don't you?"

"It's a solid possibility. Young woman twenty or twenty-one years old off at university disappears for several months. Seems likely doesn't it?"

"I agree, and the way she became isolated from her family suggests she blotted her copybook in a serious way and became *persona non grata*."

"It looks like a major estrangement, too much for a simple unwanted pregnancy," Diana suggested.

"It does, doesn't it? I suspect the Adams family is hiding something from us, but I can't force them to come clean."

"Your friend Nicole won't tell you."

"I don't think she knows, but I doubt she'd tell me if she did."

"Perhaps, I could help by inquiring at our local maternity home. Shouldn't be difficult to integrate visits with my regular duties, but more remote facilities…" She shrugged her shoulders. "And efforts to extract old press reports may be more than I can manage."

Simon pondered having another cookie, chocolate-coated ones Margaret purchased in anticipation of visits from Felicity. "I'll look after them."

"Unless Chief DeWolfe releases me from my regular duties, then I could help."

121

Simon grabbed another cookie, smiling at her less than opaque machinations. "I'll see what he says, but with summer vacations, he probably doesn't have much flexibility."

"I'd appreciate your effort, but now I should return to the grind."

Mayor Merrick called while Simon perused old newspapers in a library storage room looking for information linking George Merrick and Linda Adams.

"Detective Constable Merrick reporting," he said, chuckling. "I've talked to our lawyers and have the scoop on my father's sordid past."

"I hope, sir, not too sordid."

"But not blemish free. He either orchestrated or agreed to Alexander assuming responsibility for Felicity in 1965. Our lawyer had copies of the formal arrangement with the home, so I don't need to chase them for the paperwork."

"We should still gain access to Felicity's file, so I encourage you to talk to them."

"I can do that, but my lawyer has documentation authorizing Alexander's takeover, and an agreement saying Father would cover the costs of them taking Felicity back whenever Alexander needed them to. He also gave them a large donation about two years before he died instructing them to care for Felicity until she died."

"So, he'd accepted financial responsibility during his lifetime and beyond."

"That's correct."

"You learn anything else?" Simon asked.

"No, that's it."

"What can you tell me about his war service?"

"Oh. We had those records at home."

"Good, fire away."

"He left Barrettsport in November 1939 and didn't return until July 1945. The first nine months he was stationed in Halifax. We had train service in those days, but it looks like he never came home. And then in July 1940, he transferred to Ottawa."

"But he was military. He didn't have a civilian job."

"Correct. I'm looking at a picture of him in uniform. A military desk jockey job."

"And you can't tell me why he didn't make more frequent trips home?"

122

There was a pause before Mayor Merrick answered. "It was before I was born. I would need a letter."

"No family legends that give insight?"

"Sorry, nothing. One of those blank areas in the family history that no one mentions."

"Well, thank you, you've made substantial progress. And if you consult the home for the handicapped..."

"Yes Simon, I will contact them, but not for a few days. I have town business to deal with."

The mayor's voice had gained an edge. Simon knew he shouldn't push any further.

Simon slaved into the evening on a fruitless search for newspaper reports that shed light on Linda's activities in 1938 or 1939. Or on George Merrick's absence from Barrettsport during the war. It was after eight p.m., and he was frustrated by his lack of progress when he arrived at his apartment to prepare himself a makeshift dinner.

The phone rang after he dumped a can of baked beans into a pot. "Yo, Brian," he said, recognizing Curtis' home number on his caller ID. "What's up?"

"Nothing critical. I just didn't want to email you the results of the DNA analysis we conducted on Alexander Merrick's hair sample."

"What's the problem, trying to avoid drawing attention to an unauthorized expenditure?"

"Hey, one DNA analysis is no big deal, but you know how the accountants are. Better if we keep them in the dark."

"So, what does it show? Hang on a minute. Something on the stove I must deal with."

Simon's brow furrowed as he gave his pot a stir and added cut up pieces of hot dog he'd warmed in the microwave oven. Phoning from home and obfuscating about a single DNA analysis seemed odd. And how would he proceed? Would he now mail the results from home?

"Sorry, cooking a late supper," Simon said. "What does it show?"

"Late supper is it? Enjoy it now because when you have little kids, fancy late evening dinners will be forgotten pleasures."

"God, you're getting ahead of yourself. I don't even have a girlfriend, much less thoughts of kids. And all I'm making is a pot of beans."

"I'd better not tell Josie. If she hears you're eating wieners and beans and slugging back beer, she'll be monitoring your diet."

123

"You can assure her my diet is fine. Now, what about my DNA sample?"

"Sorry, not really trying to string you along. It's a good match for the baby."

"So, Merrick is definitely the baby's father?"

"That's what they tell me. Oh, must go. Jessica's after me for a bedtime story."

After the call, Simon wondered about the real reason for Brian's protestations about a single DNA analysis done as a favour for an officer on another police force. The way Brian truncated the call was also annoying, but he couldn't dwell on those minor irritations. Learning the hair samples they retrieved from Alexander Merrick's house showed Alexander was the baby's father made his dinner of beans and wieners taste a great deal better. It wasn't proof because they couldn't unequivocally link the hair to Merrick, but it was a major step forward.

He thought about the baby's mother and the fact that Richard Merrick provided the information Simon had recently requested very promptly. The quantum shift from early days when the families were not forthcoming to the last few days when Richard appeared overly anxious to answer his questions was puzzling. And Nicole volunteering the results of her 'interview' with her grandfather, something Simon hadn't even requested. Were they hiding something by providing carefully selected information? If so, what was it?

Chapter Twenty-Five

Simon's musings continued into the night. Was the family hiding an important aspect of George Merrick's life in the latter part of the 1930s? George, a recently married man with one child, and scion of a Barrettsport ruling family, joined the war effort from 1939 until 1945. Everything other than his failure to return home during the extended period seemed ordinary. Add the question of his sister-in-law, Linda Adams, and the missing year from her studies at Dalhousie University. He had no explanation for the hiatus. Their similar paths during the early war years linked them.

He had no real evidence joining George and Linda in an extramarital relationship. Circumstantial evidence, however, pointed him in that direction. George Merrick was estranged from his wife and son during this period and the exigencies of war provided an inadequate explanation. Linda vanished for six months at the beginning of the questionable period. Her subsequently estrangement from her family was inconsistent with an inappropriate liaison with a fellow university student.

Was any of this history significant for Simon's investigation? A child, if they had one, would have been born far too soon to fit the time frame of his investigation. But it was a puzzle Simon felt he should solve.

In the morning, Simon initiated inquiries with the Provincial Government agency responsible for tracking births, marriages, and deaths, and then returned to the library.

"How may I help you this morning, Detective Goodyear?" said a matronly woman bending over a book cart near the main entrance. The same librarian helped Simon locate the book on codes a few days earlier.

He dropped that book on a trolley marked 'returns'. "I need help with social activities in Barrettsport in the 1930s."

"If you're interested in social events and gossip, you should look at the Banner, a sporadically produced tabloid focused on the families."

Simon smiled inwardly. He'd already discovered the Banner in his earlier searches in the library, but he didn't want to discourage the friendly and helpful library assistant. "Sounds perfect, but was it published in the 1930s?"

"Definitely. From the 1920s until after the war."

"Where do I find them?"

"I'll get them for you. 1930 to 1939?"

"Yes please, and also the forties until 1945."

"I'll be right back, and if anyone returns books while I'm gone, just add them to the cart."

Simon played librarian until she returned with a pile of unbound documents on another cart.

Two hours later, Simon met Diana Jackson as he re-entered the police station. She displayed a big toothy smile.

"What's with you?" he asked.

"Access Nova Scotia called about your inquiry this morning. Margaret's wondering what you want to do about it."

"Why didn't she call?"

"No response. She asked me to watch for you."

Simon extracted his phone from his pocket. "The damn thing's turned off. What did the vital statistics people say?"

"You'll have to ask her. I'm on a call and I must get on with it."

When Diana returned fifteen minutes later, Simon had all the details the vital statistics office would give him without a court order.

He waved her into his office. "Linda Adams had a daughter out of wedlock in July 1939. She was given up for adoption. That's all they'd tell me."

"Mrs. Murphy's Maternity Home people didn't admit to it when I checked with them yesterday."

"Too close to home. Her parents sent her farther away to isolate her from the limelight."

"Father?"

"Not reported on the official form, but I do have the facility address. They could have additional information."

"You think this is useful?"

126

"That baby has the genetic makeup to be Hope's mother."

Diana held up her hand. "Does calling her Hope indicate you accept Alexander's code flag story?"

"We know Felicity was not Hope's mother, but I see no reason to question the name. And it's better than continuing to call her 'the baby'."

"But it only makes sense if you assume George Merrick is the earlier baby's father?"

"That's not far-fetched. Linda Adams had the baby in 1939. George left in November to join the war effort and wasn't seen again until 1945. Linda also joined the forces and for at least part of that time, posted to the same cities."

Diana stared at Simon's whiteboard with the latest version of his notes on potential players in the case. She drew a line joining the entry describing Linda's illegitimate baby and Simon's comments about George's prolonged wartime absence. She nodded her head. "An affair between George and his wife's sister, if it became known to the families would explain the animosity."

"And twenty years later, if Alexander fathered a child with Linda's daughter…"

"For God's sake, Simon, that's not on. What are the chances of Linda Adams' adopted baby growing up and getting together with Alexander Merrick? It's too far-fetched."

"What did some smart-ass say? Eliminate the impossible, and then focus on whatever is left, no matter how improbable."

"That was Conan Doyle, something he had Sherlock Holmes say. 'Once you eliminate the impossible, whatever remains, however improbable, must be the truth'."

"Well, I was close, and Sherlock Holmes was a smart-ass, even if he was a fictional one. I have no other candidate for the mother, so this is my best lead."

"You'll need a court order to release the adoptive parents' names."

"Yeah, that's next, and I'm already working on it," Simon gazed at a sheet of paper on his desk. "If you handled this, I could get back to finding Alexander."

"Certainly. Never actually made an application, but I know where to deliver it."

Simon handed over the form. "Good experience for you. Complete the form using this template, I'll sign it, and you take it to Bridgewater."

127

She was on her way out when he added, "Do it during your shift. The chief won't accept you spending your time on this."

Mayor Merrick called after Diana departed. He was back pretending to be Detective Constable Merrick.

"Been to the family doctor. He's received Felicity's medical files and given her a check-up. Confirms your supposition she never had a baby. I don't understand why you needed this, but there it is."

Simon sighed. They'd been over this point three different times. "Because the DNA evidence wasn't one hundred percent certain," he replied. "Now we can be sure. What about periods when she returned to the facility?"

"Twice, three months at a time. Once in 1975 and a second in 2000."

"Shoot, I hoped for more visits, and a pattern to work on."

"Sorry, that's what the records show. Anything else you need Felicity and me to do?"

"Tell her Margaret has bought a pot of cocoa and chocolate cookies, so she can visit the station anytime."

*****

As Diana expected, filling in the application to determine the adoptive parents of Linda Adams baby was dead simple, much easier than the rigmarole they'd followed in the UK. She had the job including Simon's signature finished in ten minutes. She phoned the Bridgewater courthouse to confirm a magistrate or judge would be available and departed. If it went smoothly, she would be back in Barrettsport when her shift ended at four o'clock. If not, Travis could handle it.

Travis stood in the kitchen when Diana rolled in a few minutes before five. William and Oliver, Diana's two young boys, were sitting at the table slaving over their homework. "Everything's fine, but you shouldn't let them take advantage of you."

Diana stretched her arms around her long-haul trucker's substantial girth as he slaved away at the stove. He'd complained about her willingness to put in extra hours on several occasions, always stressing the system took advantage of her because she was black.

"Not this time, lover boy," she replied. "This time I'm doing it for me. Simon will support my efforts to gain promotion if I do a good job."

128

"Yeah, but they expect you to do your normal job and help out with this other investigation. They're taking advantage of you, baby, and you need to cotton onto it."

"Don't worry. It's under control. Next week when you're back on the road, I won't have the free time. I must make the most of my opportunity this week."

After dinner, Diana took her boys to the library while Travis visited his wife in the palliative care unit of the nursing home where she lived. The days before Travis left on one of his extended road trips always made him testy. Diana was powerless to console him. Olivia, Travis' wife, was terminally ill, and he feared she'd die while he was away. Promising she and the boys would be there if Olivia needed them didn't help. Travis desperately wanted to share those last minutes or hours with his beloved wife. He lived for her doing everything she asked, he always had, and he always would. His current living arrangement, sharing a bed with Diana, had been Olivia's idea, and at times Diana thought he did it to please Olivia. But that wasn't fair. Diana knew he loved her and her boys almost as much as he loved Olivia.

Diana investigated the lives of the Adams and Merrick families in the 1940s and 1950s while her kids were safely engaged in the children's section of the library. She was probably covering ground Simon had already covered, but it would help her become acquainted with the investigation. In the morning, she'd visit the maternity home brandishing her court order. Would that call or her visit to the library yield a critical piece of information? She could only hope.

Chapter Twenty-Six

Thursday afternoon, Diana rapped her knuckles on Simon's doorframe. "I have the results of my investigation into the adoption of Linda Adam's baby."

"That didn't take long."

"Tom Kerry's my current partner. He's been good, doing more than his share of the usual legwork, so I could focus on this."

"And what did you learn?" Simon asked. He wondered why she paused gazing around his office. Was she feeling guilty about sticking Tom with their normal duties? Simon had already learned Tom was the most self-effacing and easiest-going constable—the perfect partner if Diana wanted to accomplish something outside the normal routine.

"Beatrice and Alfred Turnbull are the adoptive parents. Halifax address." She placed her printout from the maternity home on Simon's desk. "Baby's father's not listed, which is odd because, back then, the mother was pressured to identify the father. But the baby's name is more curious."

"Yes."

Diana pointed at the printout. "Linda. You think they just happened to name the baby Linda when that was her mother's name?"

Simon smiled. Diana obviously relished this opportunity to participate in his investigation, but her enthusiasm might generate unwarranted conclusions. Simon's bosses had often criticized him for speculating too much. It was time to pass on the advice.

"Does seem coincidental, but Linda was popular in 1940 so not impossible. We must not jump too quickly."

Diana leaned ahead, eager to defend herself. "It suggests they knew who the mother was, even arranged the adoption with her. And that's consistent with pictures in the Banner of Linda Turnbull, a cousin of the Adams children."

"What? I didn't remember that, and when were you reading the Banner?"

"Last night while my boys were busy in the children's section. The girl was identified as Linda Turnbull."

"That would provide a link between the Adamses and the Turnbulls that makes Alexander Merrick encountering Linda Turnbull understandable."

Diana nodded, smiling. "What's next?"

"Search for her," Simon replied, tapping a finger on Diana's printout. "The 1939 address is in Halifax. I'm off to prevail once again on friends I have there. Their kids will be happy to see me, but I might be wearing out my welcome with the parents."

"Uncle Simon!" Jessica squealed when she saw him in the doorway. She charged forward and launched herself into Simon's outstretched arms. Jessica was three going on four and highly mobile. Her little sister, Kathryn, was barely two and less mobile but just as eager for a hug from their daddy's best friend.

"Come and play our new game," Jessica said without giving Simon a chance to respond. "It's Snakes and Ladders."

Simon looked at their mother for advice. "I remember Snakes and Ladders from when I was little, but isn't it too hard for Kathryn?"

"But I want to play," Jessica insisted.

"Why don't you let Uncle Simon help Kathryn," Josie suggested. Kathryn clapped her hands together. She seemed to understand Uncle Simon would be helping her.

Simon sat in the midst of what seemed like hundreds of toys, and Jessica set out her Snakes and Ladders game. She graciously passed the die to Kathryn who immediately dropped it on the floor.

"Three," Simon announced. "Do you know what that means?" Kathryn shook her head. "You can move your little person three spaces from this corner." He placed the marker in her hand and held it over the lower left-hand corner of the board. "Ready. One, two, three." He shifted her hand three spaces to the right. "Put it down here and then it will be Jessica's turn."

131

"Wow, Simon, you're good at this," Josie said as Jessica rolled the die and counted the numbers as she moved her marker. "You should find yourself a country girl in that town you're so keen on and start a family."

"Maybe someday," Simon replied as he helped Kathryn with her second turn. It ended at the foot of a ladder. "Do you know what happens now?"

"Nooo," she said.

"Your little person climbs the ladder. Here we go, up the ladder, clunk, clunk, clunk to this square way up here."

Josie knelt down and wrapped her arms around his shoulders. "Brian told me about your problems in Vancouver. We'll do whatever we can to help you get over that experience, but what you need is a wife and two little girls." She paused, but he said nothing. "If you're okay here, I'll tidy the kitchen. Then it will be bath time for Kathryn. Brian will be home soon."

The first game ended with Kathryn victorious, and after Josie took her to bed, Simon played again with Jessica.

"What brings you back to Halifax so quickly?" Brian asked when quiet returned to the living room.

"A lead sending me searching for a Halifax school girl in the 1950s. I thought I should start with the high schools."

"Catholic or Protestant?"

"Does it matter?"

Brian laughed. "You've lots to learn about your new home province. In the fifties and sixties, they had separate religiously defined school boards, one for the Catholics and one for the Protestants. Well, the Protestant one meant everyone except the Catholics."

"The girl was adopted from a maternity home associated with the Anglican Church, so Protestant, I guess."

"Then you'll want Queen Elizabeth High School if it was someone living on the peninsula, or St. Patrick's High School if she was Catholic."

"The address I have is on Oxford Street."

"Definitely the peninsula. You should visit QEH and if that doesn't work, St. Pat's."

The next morning, Simon found Linda Turnbull's graduation picture in the 1958 edition of the St. Patrick's High School Yearbook. The standard studio photo showed a sad, overweight, and lifeless girl. Simon saw no similarity in her appearance to any of the Adamses he'd met. But he remembered the 1940s newspaper photo of Alexander Merrick with a

132

chubby Linda Turnbull. The graduation photo showed a sadder and more overweight young woman, but one not inconsistent with the happy ten-year-old.

His efforts yielded the graduation photo and the little mug shots they had for grade ten and eleven students in the previous two yearbooks but no other mentions of Linda Turnbull. She didn't play on school teams, participate in activities such as the annual school musical, or excel academically.

He returned to the Halifax Police headquarters, cornered Bill Walker, Brian's code-breaking constable, and elicited his help searching for an address in the HPD computer system. Simon had already confirmed the house at the address he had from the adoption papers had been subsumed by a military base expansion during the war years. But Linda Turnbull attended school on the Halifax peninsula. Finding her address shouldn't be difficult.

Bill learned Beatrice and Alfred Turnbull owned another house on Oxford Street from 1949 to 1977. They died within six months of each other in the fall of 1977. Linda Turnbull inherited the house and remained the owner until her death in 1996.

On his way back to Barrettsport, Simon stopped on Oxford Street.

A neighbour weeding the garden in front of a house with a For Sale sign remembered her. "Very fat, smoked like a chimney. Hardly surprising she'd died too young."

"You suggesting she was sad because she was unhealthy?"

"She was simply sad. She had no ambition, no interests. She sleepwalked from one day to the next. After her parents died, she had no family or friends. A sad, lonely woman."

"No one else lived in the house? Big house for one person."

"It was rented for a few years after her parents died, then she lived there alone. But you should know about that. The place crawled with cops for days after her death." He picked up his tools and headed toward his house.

"Thank you, sir, you've been very helpful. And good luck with finding a buyer for your house," Simon called after him before reaching for his cell phone. The call came in as Simon plugged Brian's office number into the machine.

"You better return," Brian said. "We have something important on Linda Turnbull."

133

Chapter Twenty-Seven

"What's the story?" Simon demanded twenty minutes later as he hurried into Brian Curtis's office in the Halifax City Police headquarters. Bill Walker was on his heels carrying a large cardboard box.

"Linda Turnbull was murdered in 1996, an unresolved dormant case."

Simon turned to address Bill. "You're kidding! How the hell did we miss it?"

"You asked about her parents, so I didn't search more broadly. And this happened before my time."

Brian came his constable's defence. "You were focused on the parents and downplaying its significance., We didn't make the link until Bill told me their names."

"If she was murdered, my minor inquiry has suddenly become major. It might even thaw your cold case."

Brian opened the box Bill placed on his desk. "We should review the case notes and take our story to my boss. Reopening the case will be his call."

Brian started reading a summary statement at the top of the file as Simon sorted through the normal mix of crime scene photos.

A few minutes later, Brian returned the summary to the file. "It's more or less what I remembered. A violent death, but a clinical crime scene with little evidence the investigators could get their teeth into. And the victim's life was equally barren. They followed her through school and for a few years when she had a secretarial job at King's College. It went blank from 1961 when she left King's to 1984 when she returned from places unknown to the family home. She worked in sales in various stores until she met an untimely death in 1996. No life outside her job, no friends, no activities, not even a library card."

Bill brandished a sheath of case notes from the original investigation. "It's amazing. There's not a single artifact related to the years when she was twenty-three to forty-five."

"What about the autopsy," Simon interjected, thinking of his own investigation. "It should have a DNA profile or access to samples I can use to determine if she's the mother of my baby."

Brian pulled the autopsy report and gave it a brief scan. "She had at least one child, and there should be DNA results. But Simon, can't you help with Bill's twenty-two missing years."

Simon nodded. He could help with the missing years, but he wasn't prepared to abandon his own quest quite so quickly. "But what about her biological parents? Not the Turnbull's who adopted her, her real parents?"

"Mother was Linda Margaret Adams," Bill said, reading from another document. "Grew up in Barrettsport, Nova Scotia, had a child out of wedlock in 1939, served in the Royal Canadian Air Force during World War Two including service overseas in the U.K. After the war, she emigrated to the United Kingdom and has not returned to Canada."

"Nothing on the father?" Simon asked.

Bill shuffled through more papers. "Nope. No father's name in the records."

Simon sighed. "That would have been too much to ask for. But no problem, this is all good."

"Okay Simon, we can link the girl's mother with Barrettsport, but how does that help?" Brian asked.

"My DNA results prove the baby's parents were very closely related. We're convinced Alexander Merrick is the father, and I had no possibilities for the mother until I learned about Linda Turnbull and her relationship to the Adams family."

Brian shook his head. "You have two problems. First, we can't prove the hair samples we retrieved from Merrick's house were Merrick's. Second, if Linda Turnbull is from another family, how does that help?"

"You're right about the Merrick DNA sample. We aren't positive it's his, but we're all but sure, and until we acquire an actual sample, I'm willing to proceed with it. On your second point, Linda Turnbull's mother and Alexander Merrick's mother were sisters, so they're closely related."

"But closely enough? You said they had to be double first cousins, didn't you?" Brian stopped and stared with his brow furrowed for a few seconds before lurching upright when the proverbial light flashed. "Are you suggesting Alexander Merrick's father had an affair with his wife's sister?"

"That's exactly what we're thinking," Simon replied while nodding his head.

"Then you need to put them together," Brian suggested.

"The Adams family acknowledged the existence of Linda Turnbull and accepted her as a member of their clan. We know she visited Barrettsport when she was a child. I can search for more evidence Alexander and Linda knew each other as children."

"That's the fifties, what about later during the 1961 to 1985 period?" Bill asked. Brian may have been willing to consider Simon's problem, but Bill was focused on their task.

"It gets interesting if you accept my premise of a link between Alexander and Linda. In 1961 when Linda left King's College, Alexander Merrick arrived back in Barrettsport, Upper Barrettsport actually. He lived there until 1964 or possibly 1965, the period when the baby was born."

"But you don't have proof Linda was there."

"If we confirm Linda was the mother ..."

"Okay, that's a good start, but where's Upper Barrettsport?" Brian asked.

"Upper Barrettsport is an extension of Barrettsport, but across the causeway outside the town boundary."

"You're suggesting they lived there for four years a few kilometres from his family home and were the parents of the baby you found in your church."

"Yeah, the baby is the key. The hair samples Bill collected and the similarity of his brother and sister's DNA link Alexander with the baby. But I don't have an absolute fix on the mother."

"Okay, if we can provide you with Linda Turnbull's DNA profile, it would sort out that puzzle. It would put Alexander and Linda together somewhere even if it wasn't Barrettsport, but what about the rest of Bill's twenty-two-year gap."

Simon looked from Bill to Brian. "The neighbours at Merrick's house, the one with the signal flags, might help. I only talked to one neighbour. He said an older neighbour told him Merrick lived there with his sister and a wife. If you canvass the neighbourhood or search

136

municipal records, you might find something about the wife. My guess is she was Linda Turnbull."

Bill threw the papers he was perusing onto the table. "Linda Turnbull was never married."

"But my case depends on Merrick and Turnbull being together for approximately one year. They could easily have been living together in a common law relationship for much longer."

"But you've not located Alexander Merrick," Brian observed. He'd gone from reading reports to jotting notes on a pad of yellow paper. "If we could find him, and you're right about the relationship, he will have the answers to Bill's questions."

"You could help on that front because I don't have the resources for extensive searching across the country."

"Aren't the RCMP looking for him?" Bill asked.

"They're aware of my interest in locating him, but there are no charges against him, so no idea how hard they're looking. But if your people tie Merrick to Turnbull, they might try harder."

"What do you think, Bill?" Brian said, glancing up from his notes. "Can we sell this to the chief?"

"There's a case, but will he give it to us or someone else? It would be nice to get away from the wild goose chase he has us on at the moment."

"For God sakes, don't say that in his presence. I'll stress the collaboration with Simon. That it would make sense to take advantage of the effort we've already put into it rather than have him start again with someone else. You okay with that, Simon?"

"I don't know how much more I can provide to your investigation, but if you help me find Merrick, I'm all for it."

"Then it's time to attack the bear in his den."

137

Chapter Twenty-Eight

In Barrettsport the next morning, Simon pursued his investigation of the relationship between Linda Turnbull and Alexander Merrick with renewed vigour. It hardly seemed necessary because the anticipated DNA results should unequivocally establish the link if they were the parents. But a proper police investigation demanded a complete picture that allowed for unexpected complications.

Four different time periods interested Simon. The first was the late forties and early fifties when he suspected Linda spent her summers in Barrettsport. He knew she visited, but not their frequency or duration. Then he had the period between 1959 and 1961 when Linda worked at King's College. They needed to determine if Alexander was also in Halifax. The third was the 1961 to 1964 period when Alexander lived in Upper Barrettsport. He needed to place Linda there. Finally, Simon had the years up to 1985 when he suspected they lived together in Alexander's Halifax house. Brian would investigate the two Halifax periods; Simon would handle the ones when Alexander was in Barrettsport.

He started in the Barrettsport library covering ground he'd already been over. He focused on the weekly newspaper and other periodicals documenting social life in the town. Within an hour, he'd unearthed several photos of Linda Turnbull with various other children. Those photos, spread over several years, proved Linda was a frequent visitor.

One he remembered from his earlier search for evidence of children born out of wedlock stood out. It showed Linda Turnbull with Alexander Merrick. By noon, he had several more showing the children knew each other.

After lunch, he took enlarged copies of his photos from Linda Turnbull's high school yearbooks into Alexander's Upper Barrettsport neighbourhood looking for neighbours who lived there during the sixties. He got lucky with a man whose father had been a dedicated amateur photographer. He had pictures of community activities from the end of the Second World War until the turn of the century, a thorough and well organized photographic history. His snaps taken at community and backyard parties in 1962 had three clear images of a smiling Linda Turnbull, two with Alexander Merrick.

"You've linked Linda Turnbull and Alexander Merrick," Diana Jackson said when Simon showed her the new photos, "but you haven't linked them to a baby."

"The mother might have gone away to have the baby," Simon suggested, grimacing as he contemplated the serious flaw in his assessment. "But that doesn't fit my picture."

"Hiding the later stages of pregnancy and a home birth would have been difficult but look at the size of her. Some really overweight women carry babies to term without anyone knowing they're pregnant."

Simon's mood immediately brightened. Had Diana solved his conundrum without him articulating it? "Seems hard to believe."

"No kidding. I've had two and I can't imagine carrying them to term without the whole neighbourhood knowing about it."

"But you're a social person. I'm painting a different picture of these two. Could an antisocial couple living in an isolated house have a baby without anyone noticing?"

"Leave it with me," Diana said. "It's my neighbourhood, less than a kilometre from my house to the place where Alexander lived. I'll ask around."

"But I don't want you spending your evenings working on my case."

"Hey, no problem, what better for a warm summer evening than to wander the 'hood visiting the neighbours?"

"Okay, you can search for anyone with a memory of Linda and a baby from 1961 until Merrick left no later than 1965. I'll see what the families knew about Alexander's sojourn in Upper Barrettsport. Then Monday, we can compare notes and discuss where we stand with Brian Curtis."

Weeks earlier, Nicole Adams had encouraged Simon to visit her grandfather Broderick. He was a frail ninety-one-year-old, but his mind,

139

according to Nicole, was reasonably solid. The old fellow wanted to meet Simon because the family had credited Simon with finding a suitable husband for his favourite granddaughter. Simon hoped to bury that myth, but right now, it could be helpful. Broderick Adams might shed light on the Linda Turnbull situation. He wasn't planning to grill the old gentleman, but if he had something to say, Simon was ready to listen.

"You know he's really old," Nicole said when Simon called her Saturday morning suggesting it might be a good time for the visit. "I'll check with Daddy, and if he agrees we could go over this morning for coffee. Whenever I talk to Granddad he asks when you're coming, so I suspect it will be okay."

When Simon arrived at the screened porch where Broderick Adams rested, he tried to rise from his wheelchair but failed. He slumped back into the chair and Nicole helped him get comfortable. "Thank you," he said finally, his voice hardly more than a whisper. He turned toward Simon without releasing his vice-like grip on Nicole's hand. "Corcoran is an honourable fellow. He'll be good for Nicole, help her settle down."

Simon watched her fidget as she waited to hear what indiscreet thing he might say next.

"Some coffee, perhaps," Simon suggested, hoping it would encourage Broderick to release her hand.

"Yes, by all means, fetch the young man's coffee. But I fail to see why he's in such a hurry. Daisy will arrive with the tea tray shortly."

Nicole flashed Simon a grateful smile as she escaped.

Broderick watched her go, a mischievous grin on his face. "I hope young Corcoran stuffs her good and gets her knocked up right off the bat. I'd love to see her waddling around here as big as a hippo, and a great-grandson before I abandon this mortal coil."

"But don't you already have great-grandchildren?" Simon replied, trying not to show his surprise.

"I do, three of them, but Nicole's my favourite." He sighed, drifting into a trance. "I suppose you're interested in Linda and her baby," he said without any coaxing when he returned to the present. "Poor Linda, that rogue George Merrick's love child. Alexander and I were the only ones who showed her any affection. No wonder she grew as big as a horse. I didn't even know she was pregnant. I was at their cottage one afternoon and she went into labour. Alexander and I delivered the baby girl, they called her Hope, but I guess you knew all that."

140

"We pieced it together, but what happened to the baby? We know she died and where she was interred, but not how she died."

"That I cannot answer. Linda loved her so much. Being a mother made her radiant, you forgot how terribly overweight she was. Then the poor child died, and Linda never recovered. Alexander tried to help, tried to look after her, but nothing worked. She became an automaton, no life, no emotion, nothing."

Broderick was clearly tiring, but Simon couldn't resist keeping him talking. "How does Felicity fit into the story?"

"Ah, Felicity. I hear she's home in Barrettsport. Alexander hoped Linda would treat Felicity as a daughter, and it would help her get over losing Hope. He wanted them to be a family."

"But it didn't work."

Broderick shrugged his bony shoulders. "He told me nothing about their life after they left Barrettsport. That was so like Alexander. I don't think he noticed I cared for them and wanted to help, and after he left town, he never mentioned how they were managing."

Nicole returned with the coffee, tea, and cookies Broderick seemed to cherish. Half an hour later, he drifted off to sleep. Simon learned no more.

Chapter Twenty-Nine

While Simon talked to Broderick Adams, Diana Jackson and Travis Smith, along with her two sons, William and Oliver, began a Saturday morning stroll through their neighbourhood. Their immediate destination was the home of Winston and Rose Thomas, descendants of Black Loyalists who settled in the Shelburne area after the American War of Independence. The Jackson/Smith and Thomas families represented three-quarters of the black people living in Upper Barrettsport. Diana and Travis were newcomers, but the Thomas family lived there for three generations. They were friendly, community-oriented people who would remember events occurring in the 1950s.

"Alexander Merrick." Granny Thomas, Rose's mother-in-law, said. "I remember him. One of them hoity-toity Merrick's living amongst the common folk with a woman who was just as common as the rest of us. Needed to lose a lot of weight."

"What about a girl, handicapped, Down's syndrome?" Diana asked.

"Don't think so."

"Or a baby? Any memory of the overweight woman having a baby?"

"You should talk to Ginny McLean. She was their neighbour. If anyone remembers something, it'd be her."

"Ginny McLean? Do you have an address?" Diana asked turning toward Rose.

"Yeah. Ginny, short for Virginia. She lives in the same house."

"Could we visit?"

"No problem. She's getting on and will appreciate the company. I'll give her a call, so our visit doesn't surprise her." Rose looked at William and Oliver playing in the garden with Kayla and Jasmine, her two kids.

The four were of similar ages and always got along fine. "Winston and Travis can talk their man talk and watch over the kids while we visit her."

"Let 'em talk," Granny Thomas interjected. "I'll watch the young uns."

"She's old and frail," Rose said as they walked across an empty lot to the next road. "She refuses to abandon her house, so her son comes from Liverpool every weekend to fetch her groceries and look after anything that needs fixing."

A tiny woman leaning on a walking frame greeted them. The stooped old woman with a pale complexion and sparse white hair led the way into her house. "Tea? Can I get you tea and a biscuit if Richard thought to buy any?"

"Don't you worry," Rose replied. "You and Diana set yourselves down in the sitting room and I'll fetch the tea. Diana needs help with something that happened many years ago, and you're the perfect one to help her."

Ginny beamed. "If it's old memories, I can help. But if you want something that happened last week, you better go somewhere else." She shook her head as she shuffled into her living room.

The conversation that followed was broad-ranging, with Ginny talking about many people. When Rose or Diana brought her back to Linda Turnbull and Alexander Merrick, she would focus for a few minutes and wander off again. It was more difficult than Diana expected, but by the time she left, she'd unearthed several pieces of important new information.

Diana jumped up from her desk and followed Simon to his office when he arrived at work Monday morning.

"No question," Diana pronounced immediately. This was her chance to prove her worth, and she wasn't downplaying it. "Alexander Merrick and Linda Turnbull had a baby in 1963. Their neighbour. Ginny McLean, has a clear memory of Merrick and Turnbull and the birth and short life of the child."

"That would be Virginia McLean. I tried to interview her, but she seemed completely gaga and basically refused to talk to me."

"She clearly has a problem with the police. I visited along with her neighbour Rose Thomas, and we had no trouble."

Simon laughed. "The black mafia at work."

143

God, Diana thought, if Travis heard Simon say that, he'd have been livid. Diana understood Simon better. He had an easygoing way of avoiding causing offence, something he might have learned growing up in northern British Columbia where there were many First Nations people. But she couldn't let him escape scot-free. "There aren't many of us, so we must stick together. And you shouldn't be making such comments."

"Sorry, you know I meant no disrespect. It's just that your enthusiasm caught me by surprise."

"That's because I'm proud of what I learned. Rose is a frequent visitor to Mrs. McLean's, and we had no trouble. Her memory of old events is good. There's no problem with the veracity of her statements."

"Okay, what did you learn?"

"That Merrick and Turnbull lived in Upper Barrettsport from 1961 to 1964 as we already knew. The baby was born at home in August or September 1963 and only lived for a month or two. Merrick had little interaction with the neighbours but Linda Turnbull was more outgoing, enthusiastic about the baby, and distraught when she died."

"Did she mention doctors visiting or an investigation after the baby died?"

Diana shook her head. "Ginny was not forthcoming about anything related to civic authorities. People in that neighbourhood often had difficulties with the RCMP. She shrugged her shoulders and said nothing when I asked her what happened after the child died."

"That might explain why she wouldn't to talk to me, but we can't dwell on old animosity between the residents and the RCMP. What you've told me confirms information I received Friday from Broderick Adams and fills in important details. Broderick was particularly vague when it came to dates. But what about Felicity? Did Mrs. McLean mention Felicity?"

Diana's shoulders slumped, her enthusiasm diminished by Simon's statement. "You already discovered this?"

"Much of it, but don't feel your input is less useful. Confirming statements we receive is important, and your witness gave us added detail. Now, what about Felicity?"

"I asked her about Felicity, and she was adamant. No one else lived there, definitely not a girl with Down's syndrome."

"That's interesting because Broderick Adams knew Felicity lived with Alexander. If she didn't live with them in Upper Barrettsport, how did he find out?"

"Perhaps he learned about it from Alexander's father. They would have been neighbours and more or less contemporaries, George Merrick might have confided in Broderick Adams."

"Possibly, but Broderick Adams showed little respect for George Merrick."

Later Monday morning, Diana and Simon filled Brian Curtis in on their discoveries, and Brian reported on his own. He placed Alexander Merrick in the King's College School of Divinity for the 1959/60 and 1960/61 school years but discovered he did not finish his second year, dropping out during the spring term. He reported no progress on the 1965 to 1985 period but acknowledged analysis of Linda Turnbull's DNA sample was in the pipeline. Results were expected Tuesday.

He kept his biggest piece of news for last. The Ontario Provincial Police had located Alexander Merrick in a small-town nursing home facility in eastern Ontario not far from Montreal. Alexander had specifically asked to talk to Simon.

Simon packed a bag and hit the road before eleven.

When Simon disappeared for several days travelling to Ontario, he left Diana with an uncomfortable task. How could she approach Broderick Adams and learn how he knew Felicity lived with Alexander? Simon had an in with the Adams family via his friendship with Nicole, and he'd made inroads into the Barrettsport exclusive social structure. He was also a detective and a welcome newcomer to the force.

Those advantages hadn't helped Simon answer the question he'd left her. How would she, a mere constable, and a black immigrant to boot, breach the ramparts of the Barrettsport families and discover one of their secrets?

Breaching the ramparts was surprisingly simple. At Chief DeWolfe's suggestion, Diana simply picked up the phone and called Selectman David Adams, Nicole's father, and Broderick's son. Once she explained the problem, he welcomed her visit.

David laughed a friendly laugh full of merriment. "Come to tea. We'll see how Dad reacts to your presence and the questions you have for him."

Diana expected an officious butler, but when the door opened, Selectman Adams greeted her. "Welcome, come this way. There's no point in offering you coffee or tea because Dad expects us to join him for tea and biscuits. He's already treating this as a social occasion, not the first time we've been visited by the police during a formal inquiry."

"Sir? I thought Detective Goodyear had been here once or twice."

David laughed again. "He sneaks in the servant's entrance accompanied by Nicole. This is the first time we've seen the majesty and power of an official police presence."

"Now I'm certain you're teasing me, and Chief DeWolfe did warn me. But seriously, sir, we have a simple question we need help with. How did your father know Felicity lived with Alexander? Were you aware of this? No one else we've talked to admitted to knowing."

David Adams stopped abruptly in the foyer of his mansion, his brow furrowed and his head cocked to one side. "I agree. It's a puzzle, and no, I don't have the answer. If Richard Merrick did, he would have told me."

David shook his head and glanced down a side passageway before leading the way through the house to a sunroom overlooking the harbour. Broderick Adams waited for them, sitting in his wheelchair. His eyes were focused on the maid with tea tray who followed Diana and Selectman Adams into the room. Broderick showed no surprise upon seeing the uniformed black female constable who preceded her.

After some idle chat, Diana posed her question.

"Felicity," Broderick replied, gazing around the room. "I remember Felicity, but did I tell Detective Goodyear Felicity lived with Alexander. I can't remember doing so." He paused, sipping his tea. "Ah. You should ask Nicole. I'm sure she was here when I talked to Detective Goodyear. She will remember."

Diana tried, but she couldn't jog his memory. On the way out, she asked David Adams if he could explain.

"He's very old. Some days he's quite lucid, but during others he's like he was today, unable to focus. I'll ask him another time, and if I can get a more comprehensible answer, I'll call. In the meantime, you could ask Nicole."

Diana paused at the door. "Yes, sir, I will do that. And thank you for being so welcoming."

On the way to the station, she stopped by St. Georges Church. Nicole Adams could not remember anything her grandfather said about Felicity Merrick. Diana was disappointed. Her effort to discover how Broderick Adams learned about Alexander Merrick's relationship with Felicity was a failure.

146

Chapter Thirty

Simon anticipated a fourteen-hour road trip to Alexander Merrick's refuge in the small Ontario town one hundred kilometres west of Montreal. If he made it through New Brunswick and into Quebec on the first day, he could reach his destination by noon on the second. Then, if he conducted his interview Tuesday afternoon, he'd have three days for a more leisurely return to Nova Scotia.

At eight p.m. when he checked into the motel, Simon discovered the combination bar and restaurant in the motel had adult entertainment. He'd noticed bars with large signs announcing 'XXX Danseuses Erotique' along the road once he reached Quebec but didn't expect to find dancers in the motel restaurant. It was too late to dine elsewhere, so he chose a table far from the stage and settled in with a beer. He generated notes for the next day's interview while he waited for his meal.

The music and noise from the crowd made concentration difficult. Thoughts of his social life in Barrettsport soon displaced work. Margaret, when she cornered him before he left the office, suggested he was crazy to risk missing the latest summer garden party. He'd shrugged his shoulders, 'what's the big deal? It's only a party', but he understood her perspective. The garden parties were more than summertime get-togethers; they were central planks in Barrettsport's social order. But all was not lost. If everything proceeded according to plan, he could combine work with a little exploration of the Maritime Provinces and return before the weekend.

The strippers toiling on the makeshift stage reminded Simon of the Canada Day party, and the antics Josh and Nicole insisted happened around the pool. The contrast between the false smiles on the women in the bar and the delight Nicole and Beverly expressed was marked. It said something about the combination of responsibility, almost *noblesse oblige* the family members felt, and their freedom to do whatever they wanted. That freedom included the young women teasing the young men, something they could do without fear of consequences. It was a cocooned environment, a strangely utopian place, but one with serious constraints. Young people had circumscribed roles. Nicole, for example, had few lifestyle choices if she wished to remain part of the group, and she had many social obligations, obligations Alexander Merrick could never fulfill.

Simon returned to his room wondering how he would fit in. Obviously not as the husband of a family member, but as part of a lower tier with fewer responsibilities. Did he want to marry and live on the fringes of this almost feudal society? Could he happily raise kids there? Unanswerable questions, but interesting ones to ponder as he fell asleep.

In the morning, he hit the road early, reviewing the questions he needed to ask Alexander and wondering how he should approach the interview. Should he take a non-confrontational, conversational approach and determine what Merrick would tell him voluntarily? Or should he immediately trash Alexander's signal flag confession and demand an explanation?

Simon found the nursing home in a secluded location outside a small town along the highway between Montreal and Ottawa. He noticed the large church adjacent to the home when he arrived in mid-afternoon. He'd suspected Alexander Merrick would end up at a facility with close ties to a church, and it looked like he'd guessed correctly.

"Ah, Detective Goodyear, welcome to St. Stephen's Retirement Home," a middle-aged woman who identified herself as facility manager Margaret Macklin said when Simon introduced himself. "Mr. Merrick has been ordering us about like skivvies. He insists you cannot meet in his room. What type of meeting place do you require?"

"Nothing special. Anywhere Mr. Merrick and I can talk in peace would be fine. We don't need a private room. In fact, I'd prefer a quiet corner of a larger room."

"Then I have the perfect spot. Come with me and I'll show you. If you agree it's suitable, I will fetch Mr. Merrick."

Simon scanned the table and armchairs in an alcove off a large, sparsely occupied, common room. Sunlight slanting into the space

148

provided natural light. "Ideal. But before you go, what can you tell me about his health?"

"He's strong enough to talk to you without risking his health if that's what you're wondering, and there's nothing wrong with his mind. He's not old by our standards and less frail than most residents. If you want the official word on his medical condition, you should talk to Dr. Withers."

"Will he be here this afternoon?"

"Until four or four-thirty. I'll tell him you want an appointment. Now, I'll have a nurse fetch Mr. Merrick."

A few minutes later, a young woman arrived pushing Alexander Merrick in a wheelchair.

Merrick rose from the wheelchair and slid into an armchair as Simon finished setting up his tape recorder. He showed no signs of mobility issues. "Greetings, Detective Goodyear, I see you've finally found me,"

"You've caused us a great deal of trouble, wasted much time and money, and made life difficult for your family. Why didn't you come forward and save everyone the aggravation?" Simon demanded.

"Why should I? Richard has prospered, lived his chosen life in that God-forsaken town, so I needn't worry about him. Felicity was my concern, and I gave her a good home for forty-three years. Now, when I can no longer look after her, I've given her into Richard's care. It's up to him to provide her with the life she deserves. My conscience is clear."

Simon took a deep breath as he struggled to suppress his rising anger. "Your conscience shouldn't be clear. You may have been, directly or indirectly, responsible for the death of an infant. You failed to report her birth and death, and you illegally disposed of her body. I could have you arrested on any of these charges."

"No judge would allow such an action, and even if he did, it could not be enforced outside Nova Scotia." Alexander leaned back with his hands steepled in front. His religious posture reminded Simon of Reverend Leslie. "You can sit listen to my story or try to procure your warrant. It's up to you."

Simon paused, considering the best way to proceed. He decided to let Alexander spin his yarn without revealing what he knew. "Fine, tell me your story."

"It began with Linda Turnbull," Alexander said, still hiding behind his placid religious pose. Immediate mention of Ms. Turnbull surprised Simon, and he struggled to keep his own expression neutral. "Do you know about Linda?" Alexander asked.

149

"Her name came up in our investigations."

"I befriended her while I was a student at King's College in Halifax. You're aware of King's College?"

"Yes, University of King's College, a liberal arts school with Christian roots associated with Dalhousie University."

"Much more closely associated with the Anglican Church in 1958. I studied religion, and Linda worked in the administration. I remembered her from years earlier when she visited the Adamses during the summer."

The statement reminded Simon of the pictures he'd copied from the town's weekly newspaper. "So, you and Linda go way back," he said hoping it would encourage Alexander to explain their relationship.

He ignored Simon's comment. "I left King's Divinity School at the end of 1960. They had nothing to offer me. I rekindled my childhood friendship with Linda and we returned to Barrettsport. We lived in Upper Barrettsport for four years. Did you unearth that?"

"Old neighbours remembered you."

"I'm surprised any of them are still around."

Simon didn't mention Mrs. McLean or the memories recorded on film. He smiled and waited.

"During this time," Alexander continued, "my father and I argued about Felicity. He eventually agreed to let me look after her, so I brought her to live with Linda and me. I told the rest of the story with Felicity's signal flags. It's too painful to repeat. I confessed to the only crime I committed, a crime before God. Linda left me as a result. I've looked after Felicity ever since, devoted my life to her, but it will never be enough. I will never find peace. You see, Detective Goodyear, your threats of jail do not frighten me."

Simon's simmering anger finally boiled over. "They may not, but that's irrelevant. You've given me a crock of shit! We have proof Felicity was not the mother of the baby, and she did not leave the home until after you moved from Upper Barrettsport. I want the real story, not the fabrication you gave us with your childish game of a coded signal flag message."

"Wasn't my game with the flags Felicity so diligently sewed a good one?" Alexander asked.

"I don't give a damn. I want the truth."

Alexander capitulated surprisingly quickly. His serene, pious demeanour disappeared, replaced by fear and panic. He glanced around the room as if looking for an eavesdropper and fidgeted in his chair.

150

The truth hit Simon like a ton of bricks. Linda Turnbull's death traumatized Alexander, and not just because he'd lost the love of his life. "Linda was murdered twelve years ago. You're hiding something related to her death."

As Alexander stared into space, his expression became bleak and his features twisted. Simon wondered if he should fetch a nurse.

"I did it for Linda. She was the love of my life, a sad, overweight, unhealthy woman, but those few years were my happiest. I dreamed Linda and I would find joy, but it wasn't to be. Do you know why?"

Simon nodded. "Yes."

"She was my half-sister. I had no idea. We had a child, a beautiful baby girl. Then everything fell apart. Hope died like I said in my 'confession', and my father told me Linda was his daughter. Not only that, Linda's mother was his sister-in-law, my aunt, so we were almost as closely related as true brother and sister. I realized we shouldn't have children; so, a blessing Hope died. But we wanted children."

Alexander's revised confession was heart-rending, almost enough to soften Simon's anger. "But how did you end up in a relationship with your half-sister?"

"Pure chance? Fate? God testing me? We had no idea."

"Let's ensure I have this straight. You remembered Linda from when you were children, and then when you met her again at King's College, you started a relationship."

"That's correct."

"You left King's before earning your degree. You and Linda set up house in Upper Barrettsport, but neither of you realized how closely related you were."

"Again, correct."

"You decided to have a child, and when Linda was pregnant your father told you she was your half-sister."

Alexander shook his head. His placid expression had returned. "He didn't acknowledge our presence in Barrettsport until a week after Hope was born."

"A few weeks later, the baby died, and you don't know how or why she died."

"That's correct. I'd been studying embalming techniques—"

Simon interrupted him. "Why were you doing that?"

"Doctors claimed I was autistic, socially inept and prone to obsessions with various subjects. Embalming and mummification interested me. I refused to accept the idea my child would just decay

151

away. Have you ever considered what happens to a body after it is buried? No, you obviously haven't."

"What did you do?"

"I embalmed the body using the most modern techniques, wrapped her in church linen and placed her in St. George's Church."

"How did you know where?"

"I haunted the church when I was a teenager. Many afternoons, I hid when the minister locked the doors. I would wander for hours before letting myself out. On one of those night-time adventures, I discovered the mysterious cabinet with the inaccessible space. I imagined finding a skeleton, so I determined to access it."

"Did you discover a skeleton?"

Simon's facetious question failed to elicit a smile. "It was empty, but I didn't forget. After Hope died, I did what I'd done as a youth. I remained hidden when they closed up for the night, opened the space, said a prayer, laid her down and sealed her in."

"Exactly how did you gain access?"

"Through the inset panels under the sink. It had been changed, but I figured it out. It wasn't too great a challenge."

"And you think the baby died of natural causes?"

"I didn't say that. I didn't know how she died, but I'm sure Linda did nothing to harm her."

"Why's that?"

Alexander remained immobile hiding behind his pious pose. "She desperately wanted a baby, and she wasn't aware of the incestuous nature of our relationship. I can only conclude it was a terrible accident, what we called a crib death."

"What happened after you interred the baby?"

"I had a vision that said Linda and I should take responsibility for Felicity. I forced my father to give us custody and we set up house together. It didn't work. Linda was too unhappy. She returned to her childhood home, and I continued to look after Felicity."

"Until this spring?"

"I was unwell, and when you found Hope's body, I considered it another omen. Time for me to move on, give the task to Richard, and make my peace with the Lord."

"So, you pretended Felicity was the mother to protect Linda's memory?" Simon suggested.

"No one would blame Felicity."

152

"And you staged the break-in so we would find your phoney confession."

"I damaged the lock and left the door open after taking Felicity to the home. Then I drove here."

"So that's your story. Can you prove it?"

"It's my story and you can accept it or reject it. It's of no concern to me."

"I don't believe it. You're hiding something and I *will* determine what it is."

Merrick shrugged his shoulders and shuffled back to his room without saying goodbye.

Chapter Thirty-One

Simon sat staring at the empty wheelchair before searching for Dr. Withers. The good doctor confirmed Ms. Macklin's opinion. Alexander was frail but not suffering from an ailment that should lead to his imminent demise. His problem was mostly self-neglect; he'd almost starved himself to death. Once they improved his diet and dealt with a few non-life-threatening ailments, he should live for a completely unpredictable number of years.

Simon walked from Dr. Withers' office to Merrick's room. He stood in the open doorway watching Alexander in a recliner chair staring into space, his hands held in front of him in prayer. Dr. Withers stood behind Simon. Merrick looked up after a few minutes, waiting for Simon to speak.

"Your story is partial truth, a carefully scripted rendition of some of the facts I need to put the case related to your daughter's death and internment to rest. But it doesn't explain why you fabricated the yarn about Felicity's role, or why you are hiding here. Will you answer those questions, or do I defer to the Halifax Regional Police? Dr. Withers says you are strong enough to travel, and I'm sure they would have grounds to extradite you to Nova Scotia."

"I anticipated your return," Merrick replied in the calm, considered voice he'd used at the beginning of their earlier conversation. "I'm tired but will explain things in the morning if you'll give me time to rest and gather my thoughts."

Dr. Withers stepped forward and made a quick check of Merrick's pulse and breathing. "That might be best. We can ensure he stays here and gets proper medical care."

Simon fixed Merrick with a withering glare, confident he now had his adversary beaten. "I want the truth, not another carefully crafted fabric of half-truths."

Before finding a motel and restaurant, not ones with XXX Danseuses because this was stodgy old Ontario, Simon consulted Brian Curtis. "Do you want someone here? He could have revelations related to your investigation."

"Record the interview and have him sign a statement. We don't know what he'll say, but I'm confident you can handle it."

The next morning Alexander Merrick handed Simon a typed statement after the nurse left him in the meeting area. He didn't leave the wheelchair. The statement, witnessed by Dr. Withers and Mrs. Macklin, ran to four pages.

"I see no point discussing this," Alexander said. "Nothing bears on your investigation. I suggest you take it to the Halifax police and let them deal with it."

Simon studied the document. It provided a comprehensible explanation of Alexander's behaviour and referred to missing women, possibly the ones in the case Brian had been investigating. "If you have nothing to add, I'll be on my way. However, based on what I've read here, I assure you detectives from Halifax will demand an interview. You should keep them apprised of your movements."

"You know damn well you cannot insist on that."

"I'm not so sure. With serious allegations like the ones you've raised, they can insist you make yourself available to explain everything. I'll get your statement to them this morning. You should anticipate a response."

"Fine, I'm not going anywhere."

Simon collected his recording gear and left the building. He contacted Brian Curtis to describe the magnitude of the allegations but was shuffled to Brian's voice mail. Next, he proceeded to the nearest office of the Ontario Provincial Police and forwarded the complete statement to Halifax. Once Brian confirmed it had been received and acknowledged they would handle any response with the help of the OPP, Simon hit the road.

He had a well-documented DNA sample that would resolve any remaining uncertainty about the baby's identity. He'd managed, with the help of the Merrick interview, to complete his narrative describing the chain of events related to his discovery.

155

With his case neatly resolved, he had time to consider his future in Barrettsport. But thoughts of a slower, more scenic drive home via the Gaspé Peninsula and north-eastern New Brunswick had been superseded. He had an obligation to report his findings to the Halifax Police. After the debriefing, Brian could worry about Linda Turnbull's murder and Merrick's new allegations about missing women.

Simon spent the night at Rivière-du-Loup, Quebec, and proceeded to Nova Scotia the next day. He arrived in Halifax at four thirty in the afternoon and drove directly to the main police station on Gottingen Street.

"You've started a major new investigation," Brian told him inside the front entrance. "Merrick has implicated one of our biker gangs in the disappearance of twelve young women fifteen years ago. This is far bigger than providing us with guidance on how or why Linda Turnbull was killed. Come to my new office and I'll fill you in."

Simon followed him into a different part of the station.

Brian pushed open a door with 'Vice' written on the glass half panel. "Starting this morning, Bill and I are located in the vice section. You should feel at home."

"Yeah, right. I can do without the vice squad. That damn raid gives me nightmares."

"Still bothers you, does it? I don't know why it should. Your team rescued sixty young women from very uncertain futures."

"Two innocent girls were murdered in front of my eyes, and I couldn't do anything about it. And a colleague almost met a gruesome death."

"But she didn't, and I heard you played major roles in a successful operation. You should get over it."

Simon shook his head. "Easy for you, you weren't there. But let's forget that. What's happening in staid old Halifax?"

"I'll fill you in, but first I need the tapes of your interviews. I'll get them copied and transcribed."

"They won't be much use. The first day we talked about my case, not yours. On day two, he presented me with the statement you already have."

"Nevertheless, we need them, and I can save you effort by having them transcribed."

Simon laughed. "And if they contain any information you need to suppress, you'll clamp a lid on it."

156

"Can't fool you, can I? Ours is a sensitive investigation involving organized crime, so we must consider security, and the tighter we keep things the better."

"Okay, I'm not fighting with you," Simon said as he surrendered the tapes. "What's this top secret high profile case I've stumbled into?"

"Be right back," Brian replied waving at Bill Walker. "Get the team together and see if someone can scare up fresh coffee?"

Bill escorted Simon to a typical police station meeting room with harsh fluorescent lighting. It contained a steel table with twenty uncomfortable-looking steel chairs and a large bulletin board across the end wall. Otherwise, it was empty except for two portable easels in one corner, and a small stand with a computer monitor and keyboard.

Brian addressed the assembled team after they listened to Simon's interview tapes. "Linda Turnbull was the mother of a baby girl who died in 1963. Simon discovered Linda Turnbull and Alexander Merrick were the parents, and he now has the evidence to put his case to rest."

A detective stated the obvious. "His investigation linking Linda Turnbull and Alexander Merrick opens a whole new line of investigation for us."

"And we need someone in Ontario to fill gaps in this crazy story," another added waving his copy of Alexander Merrick's statement.

"I understand, and we've made flight reservations for Burrows and West," Brian interjected. "But first, I want to review what we know in case Simon can provide additional insights based on his knowledge of Merrick."

Brian paused, looking around the room. He began when no one commented. "Here's the story from Merrick's statement. One evening in 1995, date not specified, Linda Turnbull observed the kidnapping of one of the nine young street workers who disappeared during that period. We don't have a firm ID from the statement, but the description Turnbull gave Merrick narrows it down to three possibilities. Everyone okay so far?"

"Can't we establish the date of this purported kidnapping?" Detective Sergeant Burrows asked.

"It's one thing we need to work on, both when you're talking to Merrick, and also on the ground from this end. But getting on with my summary, Merrick claims Turnbull suspected the people responsible for the kidnapping, who she described as bikers, noticed her presence. She feared for her life but didn't contact us. She phoned Merrick and told

157

him her tale. He claims she sounded terrified, and he hurried over to her house. When he arrived, she was on the floor, dead. He then left without contacting us. Later, we received an anonymous tip, probably from Merrick."

Sergeant Burrows stood, leaning forward with his palms resting on the table. "That suggests Turnbull's murder and the whore's disappearance were on the same day."

Brian motioned for Burrows to sit down. "Not necessarily. Turnbull could have stewed over her predicament before calling her ex-husband. They were not on particularly good terms, so she may not have contacted him for several days."

Burrows remained standing. "But she couldn't have waited weeks because the reports from the original investigation say none of her normal acquaintances noticed anything in the days preceding her murder."

"Which was on a Monday, suggesting the kidnapping was at most four or five days earlier. Perhaps Merrick will tell us something that supports or refutes this idea."

"You may learn more from Merrick because his memory seems strong," Simon suggested. "His grasp of facts from all those years ago suggests he may have a diary he'd been consulting. The diary, if he has one, would be useful because his story has been fluid. It changes as new evidence is brought to his attention, or he's challenged on some point."

"You think he has the diary in the nursing home?" Constable Charlene West asked.

Brian held up his hand. "Careful now, there may be a diary, but we don't have grounds for a search looking for it."

"Alexander is familiar with the legal situation and his rights," Simon added. "But the diary would help with confirmation of his statement."

"We should pressure him for proof that supports his various claims," Burrows suggested with chin thrust forward and his voice a growl. "He might offer the diary as proof of something he's said. Then we'd have our grounds for a search."

Simon wondered about the wisdom of sending Burrows, a throwback to tough, head bashing cops of an older era, and the young Constable West to interview Merrick. But it wasn't his case, so he didn't comment.

"Okay, that's the current status," Brian said, breaking into Simon's thoughts. "Bill and I will dig into the veracity of Merrick's story from the Halifax end while Burrows and West interview Merrick. If he's willing, I would appreciate Simon's help while we revisit some of the ground he covered in the past weeks. Then he can get back to his responsibilities in Barrettsport, and we can try to shed new light on what happened to these missing women."

Chapter Thirty-Two

Friday, Simon joined Brian Curtis's team as they assembled for another morning meeting. Later, he ground his way through Alexander Merrick's statement, providing comments based on what he'd learned about Alexander over the previous few months. Simon added several pages of other observations related to the case and presented the package to Brian.

Brian quickly scanned the documents and put them aside. "Lunchtime. Should we grab a bite and talk to Merrick's neighbours? You might notice something I miss. Then I guess we'll let you go home for the long weekend."

"Generous of you," Simon laughed as they strode from the station.

Conversations with people near Alexander Merrick's signal flag house confirmed he was an unfriendly individual who confided in no one.

One neighbour summed up the situation. "Merrick talked to you for one of two reasons. He either wanted to vent his anger about some bloody useless topic, or he wanted something from you. He never dropped by to chew the fat or offer a hand."

Brian offered his own conclusion as Simon prepared to leave. "We're no further ahead when it comes to looking back more than ten years, so I guess the next step is municipal records. And for someone who claimed to be a devout Christian, there's not much sign of Christian charity."

"No one's suggested he was ever anything but generous to Felicity, but other than that…" Simon shook his head, put his car in gear and slowly pulled away.

Simon arrived in Barrettsport at six and consumed his traditional Friday fish and chips at the Causeway Pub. After dinner, he stared into the marsh from atop a dune behind the Upper Barrettsport beach. The warm summer evening with a light offshore breeze was ideal for navel gazing about his first months in Barrettsport.

He had to love a town where he could spend three months investigating the death of a baby who probably died of natural causes fifty years earlier. Anywhere else, the case would have been quickly swept under the carpet as more pressing, and likely depressing, issues took precedence. But in Barrettsport, citizens from shop girls to the mayor cared about the child, and he had the opportunity to answer their questions.

He'd made several valued friends and earned the respect of the mayor and several family patriarchs. Best of all, he'd established a strong working relationship with a colleague, a constable with a bright future.

He didn't hear Diana Jackson, the aforementioned constable, approach.

"Welcome back," she called out. "I understand your trip was a success, and you solved your little mystery."

"You read my report, did you? I only emailed it to the chief yesterday, but I assume he showed it to you."

"That's correct. He had a question about the maternity home."

"Are those your kids?" Simon asked, looking toward two young boys who were trying to attract Diana's attention. He didn't want her to conclude he was annoyed the chief would ask her questions about his report. In fact, he was pleased Chief Dewolfe had noticed her input.

"Yeah, William and Oliver letting off steam before they go to bed." She laughed. "They'll be okay rearranging the beach."

They did appear to be reengineering the beach by digging a channel that allowed water trapped in an intertidal pond to escape. Diana waved and they returned to their task.

Simon turned to the marsh. "Thinking of engineering, would you say the town receives the value it should from this marsh?"

"You suggesting they drain it?"

He laughed. Trying to drain the marsh would be akin to King Canute's efforts to hold back the tide. "No one would agree to that. More like boardwalks built into the marsh and an interpretive centre. It could become an ecological attraction."

"Sounds like you're getting committed to our little town. Decided you'll stay, have you?"

161

"Yeah, I considered it on my trip to Ontario. I'm starting to feel like I belong."

"And your first civic action will be a redesign Cornelius Barrett's duck hunting grounds."

"Duck hunting? Isn't it a wildlife refuge?"

"Not in the old days. When Barrett, the Yankee privateer, and his cronies established Barrettsport, they wanted to shoot wildfowl, not conserve nature. When the town's population grew, they had a few incidents of people and horses getting shot as they crossed the causeway. They transformed it into a conservation area. Much later, Ducks Unlimited purchased the mainland side. Now they manage the whole thing."

Simon clambered around the last two dunes to the channel joining the marsh to the ocean. "Developed or not, it's a resource the town should promote. And what's with this channel? I'm sure it's wider than it was when I arrived."

Diana climbed to the top of the penultimate dune, a spot where she could keep an eye on her kids while continuing the conversation. "You definitely are getting attached to the place. Next thing we know, you'll be looking at real estate. But what about your case, is it really finished?"

"I've nailed down the parent's identities, and I doubt we'll learn how the baby died. So not much point in pursuing it."

"But you don't sound completely satisfied," Diana said before walking toward her boys.

Simon followed, trying to put aside thoughts of development possibilities for the marsh. "I have several lingering issues, but as I said, we won't make progress, so best to let them be."

"What problems?"

"First, why would Alexander Merrick enter a common law relationship with Linda Turnbull? They don't seem like a good match, he's finicky about his appearance and until recently extremely health conscious. He's dedicated to his causes and an ascetic person. From what I've learned, Linda Turnbull was overweight and unhealthy, and not particularly interested in anything."

"They say opposites attract, but I don't think that's the explanation."

He looked from Diana to the marsh, and then to her kids. "What is?"

"Remember the newspaper photographs of them as children? They looked happy, and that's the key."

"How can you draw such a broad conclusion from a few black and white photographs?"

162

"From the photographs and other information we unearthed, I can generate a perfectly logical picture of Alexander and Linda."

"All right, paint your picture," Simon suggested as two older boys approached William and Oliver making negative comments about their hydraulic engineering. Simon wondered if he might have to intervene, but the boys wandered off.

"Alexander was a lonely and unhappy lad. He didn't get on with anyone, other kids, grown-ups, teachers, anyone. He and Linda became friends because she was also a lonely kid with no other friends. They both looked forward to the summers doing whatever kids the age of my two or a little older do together. You know, nothing bad, just kids playing together and learning whatever they learn."

"Okay, you're suggesting Alexander had fond memories of those summers when he met her again at King's College?"

Diana nodded. "That's what I'm suggesting. They were two lost, friendless souls who remembered being happy together as kids."

"Why didn't he explain this when I interviewed him?"

"Because of his autism or whatever mental issue he has. He lives in a strange world where he sees facts but not emotions. It doesn't occur to him to describe his emotional state. He may not appreciate he was attracted to her when he was twenty-one because of their feeling for each other when he was eleven."

Simon hesitated while looking south-westward into the marsh. The sun stood high above the horizon, but the sky already had a slightly orange hue. In another hour they would have a beautiful sunset.

Red sky at night, sailor's delight, he thought as he considered Diana's assessment. "Alexander attributed the attraction to divine intervention, but your explanation makes more sense."

"His religious take is consistent with the psychological profile I'm generating. Anyway, I suspect that's why they reunited, and the photos when they lived here in the 1960s are consistent. They also showed a happy couple."

"And nothing Merrick said contradicts anything you've suggested. So, you're on a roll. Now you can eliminate my other big question mark."

"And it is?" Diana asked as she examined a piece of flotsam Oliver dug from the sand.

"Can we unequivocally attribute the baby's death to Alexander Merrick, George Merrick or Linda Turnbull?"

"What's your case against Alexander?"

163

"He admits learning Linda was his half-sister devastated him, and he's aware of biological and theological reasons for opposing people in their circumstance having a child."

"You're suggesting he was disgusted and despondent and killed her?"

"All we have to refute it is his statement, and we know he's lied repeatedly."

"But he wouldn't have treated the body in such a reverential way."

"Perhaps he did it to hide the evidence," Simon suggested as Diana began gathering up trowels and rakes her boys brought with them.

"I don't think so. There must be less risky ways to dispose of the body. I'd argue the treatment of the body and his efforts to maintain their life together aren't consistent with killing the baby in disgust."

"Could be. Now, what about Linda?"

"What's your scenario suggesting she murdered her baby?"

"Perhaps she learned what George told Alexander about them being siblings. She was disgusted by the nature of their relationship and despondent. And we know Linda never recovered."

"Possible, but more likely she was despondent because the baby died and never recovered. You have no proof, and it will be the same for a suggestion George Merrick was incensed at their behaviour, lost control and did in the baby."

"That's my problem. We can't prove a case against any of them."

"And you can't even say it was murder," Diana observed.

Simon sighed as he ran his hand through his hair. Their discussion of the case had reached the same conclusion he'd reached previously. They'd determined the baby's parents but hadn't resolved many other issues.

"I can't, and that's why I must close the file. We'll get the results from Alexander Merrick's and Linda Turnbull's DNA samples, and if there are no surprises, we'll put it to bed. I'll never make a case. All I have is disposal of the body, and Alexander admitted to that. Unless Alexander implicates the others, there's nothing there for me."

"And both of them are dead. So, you'll be in the office next week to wrap this up?"

"Tomorrow, but not until afternoon. I'll be busy in the morning. More of my deepening commitment to my life in Barrettsport."

"Ah, designer furniture for your apartment?"

"Nothing like that. Just a trip to buy stuff for my kitchen, and a new resolve to stop eating so many meals at the Causeway Pub."

Diana smiled. "And where did you eat tonight?"

164

"At the pub, but I had no food in my apartment. Now, shouldn't we check up on your kids?"

Diana corralled her two boys and the four of them strolled toward Upper Barrettsport. Simon sensed there was also uncertainty in Diana's mind as they approached her house.

Chapter Thirty-Three

Diana addressed her boys as they entered her small house. "You guys go play a quiet game while Detective Goodyear and I have tea."

"It's nice," Simon said, glancing through an archway into a combined living-dining room.

Diana laughed as she filled the kettle, "Bit of a pigsty if you ask me, but what can I expect with two boisterous young boys."

"It's nice and homey like people actually live here."

"I can imagine your bachelor stud apartment. Homey and lived in don't leap to mind."

"Empty and sterile describes my place. I haven't furnished most of it, and I'm at a complete loss when it comes to the stuff that makes it feel like home."

"Don't let that bother you. Making like a home decorator and trying to buy those things never works. You acquire those mementos gradually. You can start next month with something that reminds you of Nicole and Josh's wedding."

"Why would I especially commemorate that? Nicole's been a friend and generous with her time, and Josh seems like a good sort, but it's only the wedding of relatively new friends."

Simon watched Diana as she fussed with the teapot. Was it possible for someone whose skin was the colour of pitch to blush? He swore she was blushing.

Diana placed the teapot and two cups on her kitchen table. "I don't understand why Alexander Merrick accused his sister of being the baby's mother."

"Are you changing the subject?"

166

"No. Well, yes I am. You'll find out at the Natal Day garden party. I really mustn't say anything. So, why did he do it?"

"Why did he spin the yarn about Felicity being the mother?"

"Yeah. Such an elaborate ruse, all those flags and all that effort."

"That was a puzzle until my second day in Ontario. Alexander produced a statement that cleared everything up. The Halifax police are working on the details and a bunch of implications."

"Not in your report to the chief."

"HPD is keeping the lid on this because the case involves organized crime and biker gangs. It's confidential."

"If you'd rather not tell me I'll understand."

"I'm filling the chief tomorrow afternoon. You're part of the team, so no reason to exclude you, but it's not something we can talk about."

"If you're sure."

Simon smiled. Her need was palpable. She wouldn't abandon her quest if he didn't tell her. "The statement Merrick made Wednesday morning claimed Linda Turnbull observed a young woman, a sex trade worker, being abducted by members of a biker gang. Linda's body was discovered a few days after the alleged abduction. Merrick claimed the bikers murdered Linda and threatened him and Felicity with a similar fate if they said anything."

"He intended to divert our attention, hoping we wouldn't learn Linda Merrick was Hope's mother, and that would keep this whole story from coming to light?"

"Yeah, that's basically the story. It took Alexander four pages, but that's the story."

"Do you believe him? The entire case has been littered with lies from Alexander Merrick."

"They're working on it in Halifax, and I trust we'll have a role if anything relates to Barrettsport."

"And nothing else takes precedence when it comes to your time," Diana said as she poured the tea.

"Yeah, that's an ongoing consideration, but all we've had are break-ins and the odd kid smoking dope. And merchants squabbling over signboards blocking the sidewalk."

"God, don't tempt fate by suggesting you're yearning for more serious crimes. You might just get your wish and live to regret it. But really, can sleazy bikers threatening Merrick many years ago explain his recent activity?"

"It does seem far-fetched, but can you suggest a better explanation?"

"He wanted to protect his memory of Linda and not bring their relationship into question."

"I can't buy that. He was too devoted to his sister to cast her to the lions so to speak for such a trivial reason. I'll put my faith in the biker theory and rely on Brian Curtis and his colleagues to generate the proof."

Simon stuck with the resolve he expressed to Diana the previous evening. After his Saturday morning run to North Point, he spent an hour at the home centre by the highway augmenting his meagre supply of pots, pans, and kitchen utensils. Despite what Brian had said, he actually did have an adequate supply of plates. He then stopped at the nearby supermarket and loaded his car with the largest quantity of groceries he'd purchased at one time.

He was in his apartment kitchen trying to decide where he would store everything when a call from Chief DeWolfe rescued him.

"I received a message from the head of detectives in Halifax while I was rereading your report. I'd appreciate an update."

"Everything related to my case is in the report, and I left Halifax yesterday before their renewed investigation got underway."

"Nevertheless, I'd appreciate an opportunity to go over this before we resume our weekly routine on Tuesday."

Simon thought he probably wanted a briefing before Barrettsport's elders grilled him at Monday's Natal Day party. He scanned the pile of groceries destined for the fridge or freezer. "No problem, I'll be there in half an hour."

Margaret Summerville waylaid Simon when he strolled into the station. He was surprised to see her, expecting no one but the constable who'd pulled Saturday afternoon duty.

"How was the Gaspé?" she asked as he strode by her desk. He'd told her before he left that he planned a more leisurely drive home via the Gaspé Peninsula, visiting Percé Rock and other geographic icons.

"Never made it to the Gaspé," he replied. "The trip was interesting, but I expected more farms and villages and less forest primeval."

"It depends on where you go. There are areas like you imagine along the shores of the St. Lawrence and in southern Ontario, but if you look at Google maps, it's mostly forest."

"You're right and I guess I already knew that but driving brought the story home."

"So, the trip was worth it?"

168

"Yeah, my case is solved. I'll tidy it up, and everyone can get on with their lives. But Diana hinted about developments around town. What have I missed?"

"Lots," she replied, leaning back with a teacup in her hand. He wondered again what brought her into the office. "Nicole's wedding date has been announced. They're going on a long cruise, delivering the boat Josh just finished to Europe. They're also having a modern-looking house built in Hunter's Creek, and Jim Ellis will be in charge of the project."

"I didn't know Mr. Ellis was a builder."

"Apparently he oversaw large construction projects."

"A civil engineer or something like that. Well good for him. He's decent and knowledgeable, but self-effacing. He insisted he was a rough carpenter, while in truth, he's a bleeding expert."

"Josh was looking for you, and he showed me the plans."

"A big house?" Simon asked. Family members choosing to live in Hunter's Creek was interesting. It suggested their exclusiveness with parties on their big Barrettsport estates might be unravelling.

"Not very big, but I'm not sure how to describe it. You'll have to see the plans. It doesn't look anything like the buildings in the Creek, but it looks like it will fit right in."

"So, why was he looking for me?"

"He didn't say, but my spies tell me he will ask you to be best man at the wedding."

"Me! Doesn't he have a buddy from New England? How can I be best man? I've only known him for a couple of months."

"It's an honour. You should be pleased he's asking you. It almost makes you a member of the families."

"Hardly," Simon laughed. "Anything else happen?"

"The chief wants to see you."

"Yeah, I know. That's why I'm here."

169

Chapter Thirty-Four

Simon poked his head into Chief DeWolfe's office, and the chief immediately grabbed his hat. "A celebration is in order, and anyway, this place is as busy as Grand Central Station."

He led the way past one constable discussing something with a citizen and a second in animated conversation with Margaret. On Second Avenue, he turned toward town saying nothing until they entered the Traveller's Inn bar.

"Anything else to add to the report you forwarded to us on Thursday?" Chief DeWolfe asked as he threw his hat onto a bench.

Simon sat pondering the meaning of their trip to the inn. Why was the chief revisiting the telephone discussion they had half an hour earlier? "I think I covered the facts."

"The prosecutor's office wants closure. Provide them the baby's identity and your explanation of how she arrived in the sacristy and close the file."

"You suggesting we take Alexander Merrick's latest confession at face value and call an end to the investigation?"

"We have no choice," the chief stated before turning to the waitress. "Keith's draft for me, a large one. And you Simon?"

"Garrisons Red if you have it on tap," he said to the waitress before turning to the chief. "My friend Brian and his buddies on the Halifax force were raving about it, so I'm giving it a try."

"Craft beers, they're all the rage these days, but some are odd. That one, I'd agree with our Halifax colleagues, it's quite good. Now, Alexander's statement, can you find any holes in it?"

170

"I tried to develop ways of testing his assertions but came up with nothing tenable, and his story is consistent with several facts I withheld." Simon shrugged his shoulders, thinking about similarities with the previous evening's discussion with Diana. "I guess this is as close to certain as we'll get."

"And we've identified the baby's parents?"

"All but certain—Alexander Merrick and Linda Turnbull. We'll have the DNA results to confirm it in a few days."

"And how she died?"

"The autopsy report reached no conclusion. We won't learn any more."

"And how she arrived in the cupboard?"

Simon hesitated as the waitress plunked two large beer steins on their table. He wondered where the chief was headed. He was reviewing basic facts clearly documented in Simon's report.

"Solid, if we accept Alexander's statement and Josh Corkum's evidence."

"Alexander's statement is basically a confession, and you said it fits the facts."

"Yes."

The chief shrugged his shoulders. "That's the story we relate to the prosecutor's office."

"It seems to be our only option."

"But you're not happy?" the chief suggested.

That's his plan, Simon thought. He's reviewed the details in the official report, before starting an off-the-record discussion of the inevitable loose ends. Simon glanced around the almost empty bar. The chief had chosen his opportunity to address issues that would never be part of the official record.

"We have the sordid story of George Merrick's affair with his sister-in-law. And we can't determine the extent of George Merrick's involvement in the cover-up."

"Between us, what did you conclude?"

"I put the bare outline in the report. An affair between George Merrick and Linda Adams producing the baby Linda gave up for adoption is the only answer consistent with the DNA evidence."

"I agree. That's in the report."

Simon stopped for another swig of beer. He wished the chief would leave the unmentioned details alone. Questions remained, but they would never resolve them. "I didn't put details in my report because it's

171

based on inference and supposition. It goes like this. George started an affair with Linda while his wife, Linda's sister, was pregnant. The affair lasted for several years and along the way, Linda became pregnant."

"Why do you claim it lasted so long?"

"Stuff I read in the Banner. It implied George's marriage was rocky during this extended period. Also, the way Linda was exiled suggests this was not a passing fancy."

"Okay, then what?"

"The Merrick and Adams families did what the Barrettsport families do, they hushed everything up and produced a solution that included an arranged adoption for Linda's baby. George and Linda immersed themselves in the war effort and the whole situation blew over."

"After the war, George and Elizabeth Merrick reconciled, and Linda moved to England," the chief suggested. "Couldn't you simply argue these developments were a consequence of disruptions caused by the war?"

Simon stared at the chief considering his next words. "It was more than the war."

"The war plus a larger-than-life family drama, that's what you're telling me."

"That's basically the story until 1962 or 1963, when George Merrick became embroiled in his estranged son Alexander's life, eventually agreeing to let him assume responsibility for Felicity."

"But you can't prove George was complicit in the baby's death or the disposal of her body, and that's what we're investigating."

"I agree, it's a dead end, and nothing's in the report."

"You have other concerns," the chief suggested.

"The question of probability. The chance of Alexander Merrick establishing a romantic relationship with his half-sister was slight, and George had to realize who Linda was after she and Alexander got together in 1961. My explanation doesn't hold water unless George refrained from saying anything."

"What did Sherlock Holmes say? Once you eliminate the impossible, whatever remains, however improbable, must be the truth."

"Diana Jackson quoted the same passage when we discussed this. It's not entirely chance. The Turnbulls knew who their adopted baby's mother was, and the Adamses knew little Linda's identity."

"Why do you say that?"

"Because Linda Turnbull visited the Adamses every summer when she was a child, and she was accepted as a relative."

172

The chief help up a hand to interrupt Simon's narrative and pushed his stein across the tale obliterating water rings while he thought. "She might have been a more distant relative."

"That's what I thought when I found newspaper pictures of kids that included Linda Turnbull. They called her a cousin of the Adams children, but I didn't realize the significance until much later."

"Would George Merrick have known this girl was his love child?"

"I can't say, but you understand the families better than I do. Could George accept his illegitimate daughter showing up here as an Adams cousin without reaction?"

"May seem strange, but I can believe it, and also that Elizabeth would accept it."

"That would explain my second coincidence."

"And how George knew he must intervene."

"But he didn't become involved until they had a baby. Why didn't he act sooner?"

The chief looked up and tapped a finger against his chin. "Alexander befriended Linda when they were children, met her again by chance ten years later. Not such a big coincidence. The question is, when did Alexander learn the sordid details, and could his knowledge have affected his actions before the baby died?"

"I don't think he realized who Linda's parents were until his father told him after the baby was born, or even after she died."

"Why not?"

"Because his religious convictions would never have allowed him to contemplate having a child with someone who was essentially his sister. He could not have learned before the baby was conceived."

"You're suggesting George told Alexander nothing until late in the pregnancy or after the baby was born?"

"After the birth. We have independent evidence showing no outsiders knew of the pregnancy before the birth, and Alexander would not have confided in his father."

The chief sat back cradling the last of his beer. "George is long gone, so no point in pursuing him, and you will not prove anything against Alexander unless he confesses."

"That's it, nowhere to go. An annoying loose end, but the case is closed."

The chief raised his glass, he clearly wasn't concerned about unanswered questions. "That's why we're here, to toast the successful

173

completion of your first case. And Monday, you'll attend the Adams's party?"

"Nicole invited me, and since I'm back from Ontario with no other commitments, I should attend."

"Good, that should bring more opportunities to raise a glass to your health. Now, can I get you another before I return home to deal with whatever Marge has on my plate for this afternoon?"

Simon declined the chief's offer but sat studying the last of his beer as the chief departed. An unsavory aspect of the family's behaviour obviously didn't bother the chief. They all, including Nicole, claimed to take their responsibility for looking after the town's inhabitants seriously. They appeared to fulfil that responsibility with good humour.

But Simon was convinced they knew more about Hope's identity than they were willing to acknowledge early in his investigation. Their responsibility for the town apparently didn't prevent them from impeding his investigation. When Simon finally unearthed the truth and they no longer had secrets to protect, Mayor Merrick's good will and helpfulness returned. And it wasn't just the Merricks. The Adamses and presumably the other families must have known more than they were willing to acknowledge.

After the chief left, Simon ordered another beer along with a sandwich and fries. He sat contemplating one final puzzle, something he couldn't mention to the chief or his colleagues until he had everything clear in his mind.

Chapter Thirty-Five

Nicole Adams greeted Simon when he arrived at her parent's Natal Day party. She wore an elegant and carefully coordinated summer outfit. It was blue and white and had a nautical flair, but Simon couldn't imagine her wearing it on her upcoming sailing honeymoon. The dress was less formal looking than the one she wore to the Victoria Day party but dressier than the sundress with colourful flowers on a white background she wore on Canada Day.

She noticed him giving her outfit the once over. "No more Walmart bargain bin stuff for me. Now that I'm getting married, and to a suitable spouse I might add, Mother has a new mission—rebuilding my wardrobe. This is her idea of elegant first mate on the yacht we'll be delivering to Greece." Nicole wrinkled her nose. "Not sure I agree."

"Yeah, someone said you're transporting Josh's latest creation to Europe right after the wedding. Seems an odd choice for a honeymoon, and that get-up won't work for a fall crossing of the Atlantic."

Nicole laughed. "You must stop listening to rumours. The boat's being shipped to Gibraltar. Josh and I with his best friend Kent and Kent's girlfriend will take her to Cartagena, Majorca, and Barcelona before we hit the French Riviera. Then to Monaco and Rome, through the Strait of Messina and across the Ionian Sea to Katakolo on the Peloponnesian Peninsula."

"Sounds like quite the adventure. Will you visit Pompeii."

"Definitely, it's near Naples and we'll sail right by there."

"And what about your boat mates? If this guy is Josh's best friend, why won't he be at your wedding?"

"But he will. He's Josh's best man."

175

Simon hesitated. He didn't want to mention Margaret's suggestion he was slated to be best man. "I'm glad. From Margaret's description, it sounded like Josh would be alone at the mercy of your relatives."

"He'll be well supported by a contingent of Corcorans. And we also have a role for you. We want you to provide an addendum to Kent's address where he tells everyone about Josh's past indiscretions."

"You want me to—"

"Provide an anecdote about the afternoon when Josh proposed. We also want you to escort my maid of honour. She's coming by herself and we hoped you'd look after her."

"So, my role is decided."

Nicole did a little jig, pumping first one hand and then the other into the air. "It's my party and you'll do exactly what I say. Now go mingle with the guests. Everyone is eager to hear what you learned from Alexander Merrick."

Simon wandered into the garden imagining the speech he'd committed to. Perhaps advice to Josh about keeping Nicole away from karaoke competitions. Or maybe something about the proposal and Josh's insistence he and Nicole remain outside in the pouring rain toasting Josh's bravery. It wouldn't matter that it wasn't raining hard, exaggeration was expected on such occasions.

He responded to questions posed by the guests. Their knowledge of the details of his investigation reminded Simon of his last major concern. Alexander Merrick was too well informed about activities in Barrettsport, including details of his investigation. Someone was providing him with information.

Initially, Simon thought someone in the police department was feeding information to Alexander, but he now realized numerous people were extremely well informed on investigative details. He would have to search more broadly for Merrick's information source. It wasn't necessarily a police insider.

After half an hour fending off questions, Simon noticed Nicole's grandfather waving at him. He strolled over and pulled a chair close to Broderick Adam's wheelchair. If nothing else, talking to the old gentleman would keep his inquisitors at bay for a few minutes. He should have anticipated Broderick would also be interested in Alexander.

"How is Alexander?" Broderick asked. He was the first person to ask about Merrick's health.

"He seemed okay to me, and the doctor said he mostly suffered from malnourishment and general neglect."

176

Broderick laughed. "Not like Felicity then, she seems rotund and robust."

"So, you've seen Felicity?"

He nodded. "Her visit reminded me of the effort Alexander made looking after his sister. Everyone should be more sympathetic."

"You would have known Alexander when he was a lad?" Simon asked, hoping to keep Broderick talking.

"Quiet boy, intense; not the rambunctious outgoing youngster his father wanted. He never got on with his father, and George was hard on him. I tried to intervene, he was my nephew, and I felt I should, but my efforts were fruitless."

"But you kept in touch?"

"We communicated sporadically, mostly by letter, but recently, I've learned how to send emails. How do you like that? Ninety-one and sending emails."

"Pretty impressive."

Broderick gazed around, perhaps hoping others would also be suitably impressed when they heard he was an email impresario. "Nicole helps me, but still, I'm proud of my efforts."

"Do you often send or receive messages?"

"Really no different from the old days when one wrote letters. Birthdays, Christmas, you know, big occasions, but this spring Alexander sent several messages."

"Oh."

"He asked me lots of questions about the town and the families. Said he was contemplating returning."

"And you answered his questions?"

"Of course, one must always answer a letter, even a modern one. Coming home while he can would be right and proper. And now Felicity is living here again..."

Simon considered Alexander's negative comments about his brother Richard and the rest of the townsfolk. "Would he get along with Richard and the others?"

Broderick laughed. "I don't imagine he is any mellower than he was in the old days, but he should come home."

Simon stood and prepared to move on. "You may get your wish because the doctor at the home said he expected Alexander to soon be well enough to leave."

One more mystery solved, Simon thought as he wandered over to a group teasing Josh Corkum. Ninety-one-year-old Broderick Adams was the inadvertent source of the leak. He no longer needed to worry about someone within the police department feeding information to Alexander, and no one would blame Broderick for maintaining communication with a favourite nephew. Simon could relax and enjoy the party.

Later, Chief DeWolfe cornered Simon as he made his way to the bar. "You look more carefree than you have in months. Nicole tell you something significant?"

"Only that my role in her wedding will be smaller than some people suggested. Mostly, I'm relieved to have the final uncertainties in the case sorted out."

The chief's eyebrows raised. "You now know how the baby died?"

Simon shook his head. "We'll never solve that one, but everything else, including the DNA results confirming her parentage, is neatly tied up."

"Good, the mayor's been asking me about the oft-postponed memorial service for his niece. I'll tell him there's no longer any reason to delay."

"Should Alexander have a say?"

"Richard's already talked to him. He's unlikely to attend, but he had no objections."

Simon slowly shook his head, wondering about Alexander's odd religious convictions and how they'd been responsible for most of the events he'd been investigating. Some would say Alexander's actions indicated a form of insanity, but Simon thought they simply reflected his character and the circumstances of his upbringing. "I guess they should go ahead, but I'm not convinced Alexander will be happy with the proceedings."

Chief DeWolfe chopped off consideration of Alexander's religious beliefs. "I noticed Constable Jackson was in your office a lot."

"Yeah, she took an interest in the case and helped me out several times. She's a bright lady and a good officer with a head for investigation. We should make more use of her talents."

"That has not escaped my attention. You can tell her when you have your heads together over coffee and donuts that I'll do what I can. And you, you've also shown me you can meet the needs of the job and fit in with life in a small-town environment."

"Thank you for the vote of confidence. I'm learning to love this town."

"No small thanks to Nicole Adams."

Simon laughed. "Despite the fact she dumped me for a lowly boat builder."

"You know exactly how that worked, and I heard you'll be the boat builder's best man."

Another chuckle, someone else taken in by Margaret's inaccurate rumors. "That's one bit of town gossip I know is completely false."

The chief thumped Simon on the back as he turned to leave. "I'm sure you'll do fine. Now I must discuss with the mayor the little matter of the memorial service."

Epilogue

Reverend Leslie conducted Hope Merrick's funeral service on the following Thursday. St George's Anglican Church was packed. The officially recorded attendance was four hundred and fifty, but a hundred more stood outside hindering traffic on Barrettsport's main street.

Mayor Merrick lived up to his reputation as a successful politician. He made an impressive speech about an occasion that was both sad and joyous. Sad because they'd gathered to bury a tiny baby who only lived six weeks on Earth, but joyous because his own sister returned after fifty years.

Hope's body was interred with the other Merricks in the town cemetery. For most observers, the whole affair of the body found in the sacristy of Barrettsport's Anglican Church reached a suitable conclusion. Nothing was said about the mother's relationship with the Merrick and Adams families. The prosecutor's office declined to pursue charges against Alexander Merrick.

The Halifax Police Department's investigation of the role of certain biker gangs in the murder of Linda Turnbull and the disappearance of women in the 1990s continued for months. Charges were eventually laid against sixteen individuals. Alexander Merrick's health recovered, and he cooperated with the police as they assembled the evidence presented in court. No evidence indicating biker gang assassins targeted Felicity Merrick was unearthed. She lived happily in the Merrick household making signal flags for all and sundry.

Read on for a preview of the next Barrettsport Mystery.

Tilting *at* *Windmills*

Chapter One

Detective Simon Goodyear considered his future as he drove through the rocky terrain and stunted trees that dominated the landscape along the Atlantic coast of Nova Scotia. He'd lived in Barrettsport for five months, enough time to decide if the move was a long-term solution or an interim fix. The new job was working out well, but his social life needed improvement. He drew mental parallels between the barren landscape and the restricted social opportunities for a thirty-two-year-old single man in his new hometown. Along the way, he noticed a deer grazing near the road and an eagle, or large hawk, circling. The forest life suggested opportunities for a social life shouldn't be as bleak as he suspected. He needed to discover them.

While in Halifax for a court appearance, Simon purchased two small tables in the province's major city before returning to the small South Shore town he now called home. An auspicious move, perhaps, because it was time he accepted the move east and furnished his apartment.

The ringtone from his cell phone broke into his reverie. Simon considered ignoring the call on this warm, sunny Saturday morning with no sign of the generally omnipresent fog but decided against it.

"Simon, thank God you've picked up," Margaret Summerville, the usually unflappable woman who managed day-to-day activities in the police station exclaimed. The panic in her voice indicated he'd made the right decision.

He slowed and pulled onto the shoulder. "Yes Margaret, what's the problem?"

"Thank God, you picked up," she repeated. "All hell's broken loose. We need you here."

Thoughts of his future, and the land denuded of soil and vegetation during the ice age ten thousand years earlier, no longer held his interest. Simon returned to the road and accelerated, covering the remaining kilometres into Barrettsport in record time.

"The chief wants to see you," Margaret announced as he walked into the station thirty minutes later. The matronly woman with grey-speckled hair always had her finger on the station's pulse. She would understand the situation.

"What's up?" Simon asked.

Margaret gestured toward their two holding cells without answering his question. "Sorry, I've strict instructions to send you in without discussion."

Simon took the hint and walked a few paces toward the cells. Six topless women, two he recognized as members of the pseudo-aristocratic families dominating the town's social and political life, occupied the nearer one. Simon looked back at Margaret. She shook her head and pointed at the chief's door.

As he drove the final kilometres into town, Simon had wondered what problem demanded his urgent attention. The behaviour of the citizens of his new hometown often surprised him, so he anticipated something unusual. None of his speculations, however, included half-naked wives of the town's dignitaries in the lock-up.

Police Chief Reginald DeWolfe was in an animated telephone conversation when Simon knocked and entered his office.

"The mayor," the chief mouthed, holding his hand over the phone and pointing it at a chair. Simon nodded and remained silent while the chief stammered his replies.

"Oh, God," the chief muttered as he set down the phone. He shook his head and turned to his visitor.

"Simon, I'm glad you're back. I need you to lead this investigation so I can deal with the mayor and council." The chief paused, drumming his fingers on the desk, apparently uncertain how to proceed. "We arrested six women parading naked in the War Memorial Garden near the bandstand. One is Selectman Garrett's wife."

"Completely naked, or topless like the women in the holding cell?"

"Topless, like they are now. What difference does it make?"

"A lot. Public nudity is against the law, but topless is a grey area."

"I can't worry about that," the burly, grey-haired chief replied. "Our bylaws make their behaviour illegal."

"We should consult the lawyers. We could charge them under our bylaw, but I doubt it would stick."

"Forget about charging anyone. Just make the problem go away!"

"Okay, I'll handle it. Anything else?" Simon asked as he rose and turned toward the door.

"Constable Jackson was with us this morning. She can fill you in. And we apprehended a seventh woman."

Simon didn't question the chief's parting shot because he often ended conversations with offhand comments. But the overall message was clear, solve the problem of the topless women, and do it quickly, with no fuss. Step one was finding Diana Jackson. The tall black woman with a noticeable British accent was the small force's response to the need for minority and female representation.

According to the office scuttlebutt, Constable Jackson was Nigerian but grew up in England where she trained as a police constable. After working for a few years on a regional force, she and her husband moved to Nova Scotia. She'd been a member of the Barrettsport Police for five years.

Diana sat in front of her computer, scowling at the woman in Simon's office.

"All right," Simon said before she could complain about whatever bothered her. "If we're to sort this out, I need an explanation."

"We received two anonymous calls warning us of a protest supporting National Go Topless Day. The chief decided to put a quick end to it. He organized a response, and we arrested the six participants. They were in the Gardens with placards declaring their right to go topless wherever and whenever men can and attracting a crowd."

A noise interrupted her. Diana stopped talking and looked toward the cells. The noise died down, so she resumed her report. "We picked them up and put them in a holding cell. Have you had a look? They're still topless if you're interested."

"I've noticed," Simon said without elaboration. The station appeared to have a childish fascination with toplessness. "Why didn't someone find them something to wear?"

"We offered them rain capes when we were at the park. It's all we had in the van, but they rejected them out of hand, saying they were

184

beneath contempt. In the station, we provided the orange jumpsuits we have for prisoners, but they didn't go over any better."

"What about the woman in my office?"

Diana smiled. "She's properly dressed, so it's safe to go in there. One caller specifically mentioned her, so we asked her to accompany us. She was wearing red shorts like the others but still had her shirt on."

"Okay, what have you done since arresting them?"

"There was no sign of their tops, and they won't tell us where they left them. I suggested they might want to arrange for someone to deliver them, but they declined to do so. I've recorded the names and addresses they gave me, none had any ID."

"And the woman in my office?" Simon asked, gazing at the young woman who stared back at him.

"She had ID, so I said she could go, but we'd be around to talk to her. She chose to wait, so I put her in your office. I told her to sit where I could see her."

"I don't think we can hold any of them, but we can't let them go in a state of undress. How can we get them something they'll wear without a struggle?"

Diana directed her words toward Simon, but her eyes were on the woman in his office. "We had T-shirts made for a fundraiser last spring. What about those?"

"That sounds more like it. I'll do some fund-raising. What were we selling them for? And are we sure they've given you accurate personal information?"

"Three are prominent Barrettsport citizens, so we know them. The others are actresses at the theatre in Chester. You know the place, a small town an hour's drive to the northeast." Diana paused, pointing at a photo on her computer screen. It was from the Chester Playhouse's publicity blurb for their current play. "Those three are definitely our actresses. The address they gave is a rooming house where they're staying during the run. We were selling the shirts for twenty dollars."

"Okay, I'll offer them T-shirts stressing it's for a good cause and let them go. Do they have money to pay for them, and what about car keys and keys for their rooms?"

"Not sure. I checked for weapons and had them empty their pockets but that's all. Some had money."

"Once we get the six sorted out, I'll talk to the woman in my office. I hope she isn't too upset because I suspect we had little justification for detaining her."

"I'll be right back with a bunch of shirts so they have a choice of size and colour. Should I meet you at their holding cell?"

"Yeah. I'll see what they'll tell me."

Mrs. Caroline Garrett stood at the front of the cell posed like a Greek statue. She was in her mid-thirties, a tall good-looking blonde with the upright posture of a runway model. She was strutting her stuff in a way that her stuffed-shirt husband, Selectman Matthew Garrett, would not appreciate. The rest hovered near the back of the cell. Mrs. Cynthia Ettinger, the only one Simon recognized, appeared to be shielding another. Orange jumpsuits were piled on the floor outside the cell.

Over the next few minutes, he sorted out the actresses, selling them T-shirts on credit before releasing them into Diana's care. Simon was less successful with the three Barrettsport women. Mrs. Garrett, who claimed she spoke on their behalf, refused his offer and insisted on making a phone call.

"Let Mrs. Garrett talk to her lawyer," Simon said to Margaret and the only constable in the public part of the small police station. "But don't let her go anywhere."

Simon checked on progress with the actresses and then returned to the front of the station. The half-naked Mrs. Garrett was in a lively conversation in full view of the building's glass entry doors. She put down the phone, and the constable escorted her back to the cell.

"Mrs. G. didn't talk to a lawyer," Margaret said. "She talked to someone named Lisa about their belongings. Didn't sound too happy."

"I'm not surprised. Keep a lookout for Lisa and tell us as soon as she arrives."

Simon returned to Diana's desk and interrupted her conversation with the actresses. "Do any of you know someone named Lisa?"

One actress responded. "She's a friend of Cynthia's who was at the park this morning."

"That's what I figured," Simon replied. "I think she'll soon arrive with your stuff."

"I was going to drive them to Chester," Diana said. "Should they wait?"

Simon nodded and put three twenties on Diana's desk while looking at the women. "Why don't you have lunch on us?"

He then went to his office to talk to the seventh woman.

186

"Thank you, Detective Goodyear, for talking to me," the young woman announced, standing and extending her hand before he even said hello. She probably hadn't intended it, but it was a good ploy if she wanted to prevent him from suggesting they talk later.

"Hello, Ms.… I'm sorry; I don't know your name. But I've seen you around. You're one of our school teachers, aren't you?"

She appeared to be in her late twenties, about five-foot-nine, and thin with brown eyes and short light brown hair. Not a statuesque beauty like Mrs. Garrett, more like the deceptively pretty tomboy from next door who doesn't get the notice she deserves. She wore brown sandals, red shorts and a white T-shirt with extensive embroidery done with ivory-coloured thread.

"Craddock, Amelia Craddock. I want to tell you my side of the story before you get the idea I was part of this morning's stunt."

"Then tell me the story from your perspective," Simon said after sitting behind his desk.

"Someone I'd rather not name phoned at eight o'clock. She asked me to arrive at the bandstand by 9:45 dressed as I am and watch what happened. She said it would be interesting. When I sounded doubtful, she begged me to go, so I agreed. That's it. I was sitting there, and Constable Jackson came over and insisted I accompany her to the station."

"Why won't you tell me who she is?"

"I will, I promise, but I have to tell her first."

Simon pushed his phone across the desk. "Then I suggest you phone her."

"I've tried several times. She isn't answering."

"I can't force you, but please, tell me as soon as you can. Anything else you want to say?"

"No."

"Do you have any dealings with Mrs. Garrett, Mrs. Ettinger or Miss Campbell?" He'd learned Beverly Campbell's name from Margaret.

Amelia shrugged her shoulders. "Well, yes, because we're a small community and they're prominent citizens, but our lives don't often intersect."

This didn't surprise Simon. He was aware of the social distinctions between the descendants of the five families that established Barrettsport in the early 1800s and everyone else in town. They behaved like landed gentry and led lives separated from those of the common citizens. The class distinctions had been a central feature in the only

187

other case he'd solved during his short tenure as Barrettsport's only detective.

"What about the other three?" he asked.

"Don't know them, but I will go to their play. Do you want to come with me?"

Simon couldn't miss the coquettish look she gave him as she made the suggestion, but he, foolishly perhaps, refrained from shutting down the banter. "Not until you tell me who phoned you this morning."

"It's a deal. I'll be back this afternoon. See you then." Amelia scurried out before Simon could tell her she was free to go. She appeared too happy for the circumstances, and would she have known they were actresses performing at the Chester Playhouse?

And Simon was not happy with the implied commitment to attend the play. He felt manipulated but realized it was his fault for playing along with her game.

Simon looked at his watch as he walked over to Diana's desk. It was only 12:15; he'd been at the station for less than an hour.

"Any sign of Lisa?" he asked.

"Not yet. Margaret will tell me when she arrives."

"I wish she'd show up. We need to discuss the case. I'd even buy your lunch."

"From the way you've been throwing your money around this morning, I'd guess you've come into a fortune. If I counted correctly, you've funded our actresses to the tune of $120."

"I'm confident they'll pay me back."

"Good luck. You'll never see that money again!"

"Wanna bet? I'll bet you lunch at the Traveller's Inn they'll pay the money for the T-shirts and return any change from my sixty dollars."

Diana stood and extended her hand. "It's a bet, but we must postpone lunch. I brought food for today and you should eat while I wait for Lisa and the actresses."

"Okay, I'm off. See you in half an hour."

When Simon returned forty-five minutes later, seventy-two dollars sat in the middle of his desk with a note that said *I guess lunch is on me. D.*

A few minutes later Diana stood in his doorway.

"Okay, everything's cleared up. Lisa Powell showed up with their kit. I took a statement from Ms. Powell and our six lovelies departed. Prepare a report, and we'll be done."

188

"Sounds good," Simon replied. "Draft up what you can, and I'll finish it."

"I assume you found the money. They offered to come up with the forty-eight dollars for their lunches, but I said you'd claim it from the department. Is Tuesday okay for lunch?"

"Tuesday's great, but you don't have to buy me lunch."

"Yes, I do, it was a fair bet, and I lost."

Simon's phone rang as Diana turned to leave.

"Hello, Detective Goodyear," Simon said after picking up the phone.

"Detective, it's Amelia Craddock. I've discovered a body."

About the author:

Alan Kemister is the pen name of a Halifax Nova Scotia based scientist experimenting with creative writing. He has a keen interest in environmental science and dabbled in yachting and golf before turning to fiction after retirement. He's written a baker's dozen of published short stories and one poem. Several of these stories appeared in two anthologies produced by Halifax's Evergreen Writers Group: *Out of the Mist: 22 Atlantic Canadian Ghost Stories* released in 2014, and *Off Highway: Journeys of Nova Scotia Writers*, in 2017.

A Body in the Sacristy is Alan's first novel. He's currently working on additional adventures featuring Detective Goodyear and the fictional South Shore town of Barrettsport Nova Scotia. The second Barrettsport Mystery, *Tilting at Windmills*, should be finished soon.

Links:

E-mail: alkemi47@gmail.com

Blog: https://alkemi47.blogspot.com/

Website: https://alankemisterauthor.wordpress.com

A Body in the Sacristy, Out of the Mist: 22 Atlantic Canadian Ghost Stories, and *Off Highway: Journeys of Nova Scotia Writers* are available on Amazon in paperback and e-book formats.